Walkie Talkie

by

Wee Alfie

OTHER BOOKS BY WEE ALFIE

It's a Dog's Life

Copyright
This book is the copyright of the owners of Wee Alfie and cannot be reproduced without their express permission.
www.weealfie.com

CONTENTS

All You Need To Know About Wee Alfie
The Introduction

MONDAY
Wee Alfie's week begins with a quick early morning walk in the garden followed by a trip to the park.

TUESDAY
A special treat for Wee Alfie as he's taken to the beach. All goes well until a flock of seagulls decide to take him on.

WEDNESDAY
Mummy's accident in the kitchen leads to a trip to the hospital, giving Wee Alfie a chance to explore new things around the house.

THURSDAY
A very special day of the week as Wee Alfie has a date in the park with Wee Judy, the love of his life.

FRIDAY

Friday is always shopping day and Wee Alfie is dragged along against his wishes. He spends the trip avoiding prams and endless pairs of boots as Mummy and Daddy gather supplies for the weekend.

SATURDAY
Something different as Wee Alfie is taken to a car-boot sale.

SUNDAY
A day of rest for many, but not for Wee Alfie, he still needs to have a good empty out no matter what
day it is.

SPECIAL DAYS
Wee Alfie enjoys special days as much as his Mummy and Daddy. Some are mentioned in this final chapter.

A WEE THANK YOU
A final bit of slabberin from Wee Alfie as he ALWAYS has to have the last word.

All You Need To Know About Wee Alfie

Wee Alfie is a very special dog who was born in Wexford, in the south of Ireland and now lives somewhere in Northern Ireland, although he isn't quite sure where because he doesn't have a Satnav or a road atlas. He claims to be around about six years of age but that may not be true as poor Wee Alfie cannot count up to seven.

He is a cross between a Ruby King Charles, his Mummy's breed, and a Maltese Terrier, like his Daddy, but if you ask Wee Alfie himself, he will tell you something different. He claims that his father was a boxer and his mother was a wrestler, a highly unlikely claim of course and as silly as his previous claim that his father was a Methodist and his mother was a Spiritualist, which he believed made him a Methylated Spirit. Poor Wee Alfie.

Despite the uncertainties Wee Alfie can talk, and he can talk the hind-legs off a donkey, nice for people who love to hear his stories but not great for the donkey who has to walk around with no back legs.

This book is Wee Alfie's second attempt at entering the literary world and it has taken him a long time to write. Imagine trying to type without fingers

and you will understand his dilemma. Patting a keyboard with a couple of furry paws wasn't easy but he got there in the end and Wee Alfie hopes you find his difficult task worthwhile. He needed help if he is being totally honest.

One thing is for certain, Wee Alfie has captured the hearts of so many people, not just in his homeland of Northern Ireland, but all around the world, through his television appearances and videos. He is a Facebook sensation with, literally, hundreds of thousands of followers and he is tail-waggingly delighted that you are one of them.

So how did Wee Alfie manage to learn how to talk? Well, he comes from the magical land of the Leprechaun where anything is possible and quite believable.

When not enjoying his newfound fame, Wee Alfie loves to eat and when he isn't eating he loves to wonder what he is having for his next meal. His dinner comprises of the finest mince followed by a Bonio or a bone. Try to take his bone away and you will see a completely different side to him.

There isn't too much more to tell you about your new friend other than the fact he always sleeps on his back and doesn't seem to have any problem breaking wind. That's enough information and probably too much information if the truth be told, so that is all you need to know for now.

Wee Alfie, the amazing talking dog, hopes that this book will make your tail wag as much as the first one did and that you enjoy it as much as he did putting it together.

The Introduction

They tell me there is a huge bond between four-legged creatures like myself, Wee Alfie, and our two-legged owners. Yes, I agree there is a bond but it all depends on what you all mean by huge. Elephants and giraffes are huge, most meals you lot eat are huge compared to what you serve up to your so-called four-legged friends in a tiny wee bowl, so I have every right to be confused.

When you have friends over I have to behave myself and sit in the corner without barking. You cook a great big juicy meal that lasts all night, but what do I get? The same old same old. Now let me tell all you so-called dog lovers that your so-called best friends are well aware we're not treated in any way special on such an evening. We're just taken for granted. We're not even allowed to break wind like everyone does when watching the telly. I respect such a demand but it doesn't exactly make me wag my tail, let me tell ya.

'Wee Alfie isn't allowed treats.'

How often do I hear that when Mummy and Daddy have special visitors who try to slip a nice piece of cake into my gub?

'It's not good for him.'

Says who? I'd love a nice piece of cake and it makes me feel great when I'm not forgotten. Why shouldn't I be allowed treats the same as anyone else. I do my bit. I guard the house, I chase away cats that make a mess in the garden, I deserve some sort of reward don't I? But no. It's the same oul bowl of grub in the same oul bowl. And that's another thing. Mummy and Daddy always bring out the best posh plates when friends come round, but I have to put up with that same oul round bowl that came from the pound shop. I wouldn't mind eating from a classy dinner service at least the once, but it's never going to happen. I'm not complaining. Well, actually, I am complaining.

If you want dogs to be your best friends then treat them as special best friends. We're too easily pushed to one side when more important best friends drop by and don't think for one moment we don't notice. We notice everything, even when we're not feeling a hundred percent. A nasty cold can knock dog-

owners out and send them packing off to bed to sweat it out, but dogs are more hardy for sure. Even with a heavy cold we just get on with our lives and make a good job of our many different roles. Take a sniffer dog for example, even when they have a snattery nose and hence a depleted sense of smell, they still perform well for their owners. For that, we dogs deserve a bit of credit.

And that brings me nicely onto the subject of walks. A walk is an important part of any dog's life and no dog likes a good walk more than I do, apart from really fit dogs that like longer walks than me. Even a bad walk is better than no walk at all to be honest with you. My Mummy and Daddy don't seem to realise though that I don't need a long walk when it's chucking it down with rain. Just a gentle stroll of a few minutes to allow me a good clear-out would do me rightly. It's that very thought that has made me, with a little help, write this second book, to help dog owners all around the world. You have no idea how we feel about going out for a walk, it's just something that comes with the territory, or terriertory, so this is my chance to enlighten you all.

There are so many things you don't know about the likes and dislikes of dogs. Yes, there are clever bods who think they know the answer to everything, like why we tilt our heads, why one of our ears flops down more than the other one. Well, let me tell you now, none of them have ever asked me. It's all guesswork and I think it's high time you had an insight from a dog's point of view instead of listening to someone in a white coat with a silly pair of glasses on the end of their nose, pretending they know something about something they know nothing about at all while they take our temperatures in places that are extremely private. It's the same as me pretending I know why very stupid cats climb trees for no reason at all and get stuck, causing an unnecessary trip by firefighters who no doubt have better things to do. I suppose those same boffins think they know the answer to that too, but of course they don't. Not even a cat knows why it has bolted up a tree. They're definitely not picking apples or gathering conkers for the next cat-conker tournament. Cats climb trees because they're mad.

The animal kingdom, of which I'm part of, has endless mysteries that cannot be explained. I'm a dog so I have no idea why hedgehogs cross the road slow enough to get squashed with some of them even stopping halfway across as a huge bus careers towards them. They're definitely not on the phone, I know that for a fact, but beyond that I have no idea, so it's no good asking me. All I can do is tell you about dogs, dogs like myself and my girlfriend Wee Judy. I can tell you why we cock our heads as often as we cock our legs, or why our ears flop out of control.

So you see, to many this new book of mine will be complete rubbish, but dismiss it at your peril if you want to learn more than those dog classes by women or men who roar and shout or by dog handlers who have some kind of military way of teaching us to walk properly. I can walk properly, thank you very much. My friend Seamus can walk properly too, even though he lost a leg at the vet's. We don't need to be treated as if we're in the SAS.

The following pages will tell you more about dogs and doggie behaviour than any so-called dog-experts.

To get things started let me explain how this book is set out; Every day I go for a walk, although sometimes I run, and every walk to me is different to the walk the day before, even if I'm often led down the garden path, literally, when Mummy and Daddy want to get back home as quickly as they can because there are more important things to do than consider my comfort.

There are so many different things to see and smell on any given journey and so, with a little help from Mummy and Daddy, I have made a diary of the following one week of walkies, as simple as that. Yes, just seven different days, described in great detail from my doggie point of view. So, we are going to start with Monday and we will end up with me telling you all about THE BEST day of the week for definitely getting a good feed, Sunday.

I think it's time for me to slide off this pouffe and head out on my travels, wherever they may be taking me. Right now, I know as about much as you but I'm sure all will be revealed as we plough on through the week ahead. Are yis coming with me? Get your hats and coats on and don't forget the poo bags and treats. They're both for my use, not yours. Come and join me on walks around the beautiful countryside of Northern Ireland, with the exception of our next door neighbour's garden which could do with an industrial digger running over it to sort it out.

Monday

It's the start of the week and Wee Alfie woke up this morning curled up in a ball, his nose far too close to his backside for his own comfort. Don't think for one minute that he enjoys waking up looking at his own rear-end, because he doesn't, who would? But if you have a round basket it's obvious you would have to sleep in that sort of a round shape isn't it? Why don't dog-basket makers make beds that are long and thin, like sausages, so dogs can stretch out like the rest of us? We all love a good oul stretch in the morning and Wee Alfie is no different to us. Having said that, he's very different to us as he has four legs and a tail. Never mind.

'To be honest with you all, I'm not a morning dog. Most dogs go mental, jumping around like big mad eejits but I just slide out of the bed, on my belly on to the kitchen floor. You have to do these things in stages you know, rushing isn't good for you, as Mummy says;

'You've some bladder on ya' cos I could keep the pee in for hours.

To be honest, I haven't been in the bed for ages cos the heat's shockin and the sweat's been lashing off me. I've nearly melted. So, I've been spending most night's sleeping on the kitchen tiles. Haha, a night on the tiles for Wee Alfie.

I really wish mummy would take me for another hair cut soon cos it's like wearing a fur coat in the Sahara. She'd need to get her own done at the same time. I'm embarrassed going on walkies with her. Everybody thinks she's my granny cos her hair's gone a funny colour. I like to keep my distance in the hope people think she's not with me. Oh and another thing, she always wears the same coat when she takes me for my walkies. I'll swear the neighbours must think we're on the breadline. She's hardly a fashion icon and about as state of the art trendy as a teas-made on the bedside cabinet.'

His Mummy and Daddy slept TOO well last night, according to Wee Alfie, because he didn't get a wink with their snoring and was up half the night. For that very reason he was ragin when Daddy came down the hall yawning and scratching his rear end as usual, walking straight past him as he made his way to the cupboard where he keeps his jar of coffee, Daddy that is and not Alfie. He slammed two mugs on to the work-top with a crash and that meant one thing, the same thing that happens every morning, Mummy would be up soon too. In she came. Oh boy but she looked as rough as used sandpaper.

Wee Alfie had a funny feeling, judging by the look of her, that she worked as a scarecrow during the night. Her hair was all over the place, her jumper was three sizes too big and she had a face that would curdle milk and send any bird zooming off into the sky if they saw her standing in a field. That overnight job suited her a treat according to Wee Alfie.

She didn't say much, she never does when she first gets up, so Wee Alfie just lay low until she was in better form. Sometimes that took longer than he considered to be fair.

'Mummy's always givin off to me, I mean for the stupidest things like;

'Alfie, get down off that table...Alfie, walk beside me and stop peeing on everything in sight..Alfie, you're stinkin (you don't smell too

hot yourself Mummy)..Alfie, stop begging (so it's all right for you to have a tasty big feed right in front of me?) Alfie, do you have to lie across that door so I can't get into the livin room??
Awww, don't get me started!'

They were obviously talking about him at that moment because they kept turning round and looking in his direction. His Mummy pulled the curtains and looked up to the sky and it could only be for one of two reasons. Firstly, to make sure the birds hadn't flown back in her absence from being a scarecrow, or secondly to see what the weather was like outside. Then they argued about whose turn it was to take Alfie out for his early morning stroll. Oooooo, hello, it looked like Daddy had drawn the short straw. Wee Alfie thought about reminding Daddy that he was still in his slippers. He decided NOOOO! Why would he do that? He thought he would just let Daddy find out for himself and feel what it was like to have damp paws. He would know all about it then. That would cheer Daddy up, NOT. Coffee drank, it was time for the first quick exit of the day, nothing spectacular, just a sniff around the garden, a quick wee and straight back indoors.

To be honest Wee Alfie wasn't busting his fur to go out anyway, but a bit of acting would get the door open and let him saunter off into the garden for some peace and quiet.

Wee Alfie's days consist of sitting indoors, scratching himself, sleeping, begging, eating, being occasionally naughty and going outside two or three times a day. The first, the early morning escape into the garden was, as already mentioned, always a short trip, in fact he headed for the absolute nearest piece of grass he could find from the back door, especially on cold mornings when he would have been much better off wearing trousers and socks. However, each afternoon he would be taken for a much longer walk in the fields and forest near to where he lives. The third was always a jaunt off into the darkness if he'd drunk too much water or ate something that hadn't agreed with him, or argumentative food as Wee Alfie tends to describe it.

Anyway, the first trip out of the week, on this particular Monday morning, was about to happen. He liked the first outing of the day because he didn't need a lead as he never went further than the garden, so if he took the notion he could run off in search of rabbits or other animals that were smaller than himself if they trespassed in his garden which few actually did and certainly never rabbits. Daddy had muttered a few words in his direction and the kitchen door had been unlocked. The tail was wagging off him and the tongue had fallen out of his mouth as he started panting at the very thought of some leg stretching, limbering up for the longer walk later in the day.

Wee Alfie only has little legs, well he'd look totally stupid if he had long ones. He'd look like one of those microphones that telly people use when they're interviewing people in the street.

He smelt the fresh air and was ready for action. He was off like a greyhound, well a very old one with perhaps a gammy leg or four, one that nobody had ever betted on and risked their dosh. He didn't want to overexert himself first thing. Just like humans he had his favourite place to do his business, but he never ran there straight away as it seemed far more fun to take his time and have a look around until he couldn't hold it in any longer.

'Our garden's great, full of wee things to chase but to be honest, I can't really be bothered. I've ran after squirrels and cats before and they just sit there watching me until I'm nearly on top of them and then they bolt! So, I just thought to myself, what's the point Alfie? There they are sitting on the fence havin a good oul laugh at me. I hate them!

The best bit about our garden though is the stuff the birds drop in it, not that but other stuff, which of course I can eat, like lovely bits of pan loaf. I nearly choked on a big lump of it the other day, it was so dry. I had to go in and get myself a big drink. So this is a plea to all my neighbours. Would you please butter the bread before throwing it out for the birds? Thank you. Have consideration for others, something I think all neighbours should have, especially mine.'

He saw an aforementioned squirrel and he thought it looked like a toilet brush with ears. It was on its back legs nibbling away at something or other until it saw Wee Alfie had ventured out of the kitchen and then it ran for it's life. There was no need to really because as Wee Alfie admitted he'd never ever caught a squirrel, he'd more chance of catching a cricket ball and he'd never been to cricket match in his life.

Anyway, have you seen their teeth, those squirrels? You wouldn't chance it if you were him would you? They can give a nasty nip so he'd rather sniff a worm or a mouse, but even then he doesn't eat them things cos he'd rather have a nice bit of mince or a wee chicken fillet.

Hey, you should have seen that squirrel go, bouncing like a kangaroo into the bushes. Daddy doesn't like them because he says they're like rats with bushy tails. Mind you he thinks beavers are rats with rudders on, so he isn't always right.

Wee Alfie had enjoyed a pleasant, not too exhausting, romp around the garden, but the time had come to toodle back indoors. Daddy had been calling him for a couple of minutes, but he loved making him wait, after all, he made Wee Alfie wait while he made the coffee, so now they were quits.

'Mummy and Daddy think I must have a problem with my hearing cos I never do what they want. Of course I don't. They call and call to get me back in but I now know that if I wait long enough, they'll bribe me with a tasty treat. What's the point in going in straight away and missing out on a gravy bone? You'd be mad in the head. Anyway, I don't mind staying outside for a bit, especially in the summer if it's warm enough. It's a different kettle of dogfish in the winter, because that's when I have to hide in the bushes out of the rain for a while until they give in. It's the same result though, come rain or shine. I have them wrapped round my paw, probably all four of them actually.'

Wee Alfie really enjoyed the run in the garden and now the time had come to lie upside down on his pouffe and have a wee rest before wandering around the house for no real reason. He ate his breakfast although he hadn't a clue what it was. It looked like some milky mush, the same milky mush that his girlfriend Wee Judy suffered every morning from her Mummy and Daddy. By all accounts, she had no idea what it was either. Ah well, he ate it anyway, because if it was good enough for Wee Judy then it was good enough for him. Ach, his Wee Judy, she has the softest fur in the world and the most beautiful eyes, one brown and the other bloodshot.

It was just after eleven when Wee Alfie woke up in time to bark at the postman. It's a fun game they play every day. Alfie barks, really giving it some, the postman gives him a biscuit, pats him on the head before setting off to be barked at by the dog next door. Who would be a postman? He would. He is one in fact. This Monday morning was no exception.

Wee Alfie quite likes him really but it's not the done thing for a dog to like a postman, so he just barks for the sake of it until Daddy tells him to give over. A couple of growls under his breath for good measure and the deed is done. Well done Wee Alfie. So yes, it was the same old same old this particular Monday morning.

'Our postman is run off his poor feet delivering stuff to our house. Honestly, he puts Santa to shame, apart from the pretty wrapping paper which he doesn't seem to be that

bothered about. It's great when they're parcels for me from the pet shop but it's mostly things that Mummy has bought from Ebay that she definitely doesn't need. She's obsessed, but recently has had to cut down on her buying because Daddy's working from home now and he sees everything coming into the house. If he only knew the mountains of things that poor man has trailed out of the back of the post van over the years. She's keeping him in a job and it's a good workout for him I suppose, but probably not as big a workout as when he's chased by that big Alsatian down the road. Wow, that dog has an attitude. I'd run away from him too if he was on the loose.

The wardrobes are bulging with clothes she's never even had on her back and there's me with only 3 harnesses and one collar to my name. The world's ill divided, that's for sure. I hope things change for the better at Christmas or I'll have something to say, let me tell ya.'

It was time for Daytime TV, and oh how he hated Daytime TV. It seemed to go on for hours and hours with people slabbering on about not much that would interest a dog such as himself. He had no interest in cooking, much as he would love a tasty lasagne for a change, and he had equally no interest in fashion either. He had that collar he just told you about, the same collar he's had for years and those three harnesses. Alfie nodded off as the next item on the rubbish TV show began explaining how to use the right conditioner on your hair. Use straighteners? Wise up!

'Mummy does her hair almost every day even though she hates doing it. She goes on and on.

'Alfie, I wish I had lovely hair like you cos I can do nothing with mine'.

I had to laugh as I thought of Mummy with a big head of thick beige hair with orangey tips and bits of grass and other stuff stuck in it. I reckon she'd win first prize at a fancy-dress competition if she went as a garden. That image will stay with me for a very long time even though she's definitely looked scruffier than that at times, but don't tell her I said that.

Sometimes dogs appear on the TV screen out of nowhere and I lose the plot, barkin like a mad thing. It puts my head clean away and then

Mummy and Daddy roar at me to shut up. Do they not know that I'm trying to get rid of them dogs out of our living room? Some gratitude that is. Then I run round the back of the telly looking for them, but I can't find them anywhere. They just run off the edge of the screen and disappear into thin air. What's all that about? It must be magic and reminds me of Paul Spaniels, a famous magician when I was a puppy. He used to put a woman in a cupboard and cut her in half with a saw. Daddy did that once with a piece of wood in the garden and cut his finger. Mummy says that he's getting a chainsaw over her dead body..well that might well happen if he does get one.'

The afternoon walk was a different bag of biscuits altogether, it being a much longer journey of smells and sights. The lead went on and Wee Alfie just couldn't wait to get out, away from the boring television, maybe to meet up with old friends who were also dragging their weary owners along like huskies pulling a sleigh. This walk would be an hour of fun and freedom, (that's seven hours in dog years) and Alfie waited beside the door with great expectation.

His tiny tail went backwards and forwards like a car's windscreen wiper as the door opened and the big outside world hit him between the eyes.

Oh NO, it's ball throwing time and he knew what that meant. No matter how many times he did the good deed and brought it back he just knew it would be chucked again. He wondered what the point of it all really was. Either they wanted the ball or they didn't and he wished they would make up their minds. It was so confusing. Did the owners want the ball back anyway or were they just throwing it away? It all seemed such a complete waste of everyone's time as far as Wee Alfie was concerned. Like all his pals Wee Alfie fetched and returned, all in the spirit of good fun, but deep down he wondered why he bothered. He put the ball down at his Daddy's feet who told him he'd been a good boy whilst he patted his head, even though Alfie would have preferred a biscuit to a headache. He just knew Daddy was about to throw it again and he had little choice but to go and chase once more. Can you imagine how boring that was for Wee Alfie after ten chases and bringing backs? Of course it bored him but he couldn't let it show or he wouldn't be allowed to stay out. Hey, it was better than lying on the kitchen floor as that could be fairly boring too.

Wee Alfie heard a rustling in the undergrowth and scampered off to see what it was all about. He came face to face with a brightly-coloured fluttering object that he thought may well have been a parrot. Wee Alfie said hello but no reply came back, so it definitely wasn't a parrot. It boasted the most beautiful colours of red, orange, ultramarine and vivid yellows but Wee Alfie couldn't make out what it was as it tried to take to the sky and escape from all those curious creatures, including himself. Wee Alfie had never seen anything like it before and so he chose to leave it alone for fear of the thing having a go at him. That was Wee Alfie's first ever encounter with a crisp packet floating in the breeze. Silly dog.

Wee Alfie thought long and hard about the strange object until he set about drifting off to sleep. It had been a peculiar day in many ways and it ended with Wee Alfie snoring and breaking wind way into the early hours of Tuesday morning. So he drifted into another day and maybe another scary adventure like the one with the crisp packet.

'Talking of crisps, I'm a massive fan of them. Mind you, I never know which type I like the best cos Mummy and Daddy suck all the flavouring off before they reach my gub. Mummy says to me;

'Alfie, crisps are far too salty for dogs, so that's why we have to get it all off before you have any'.

I thought to myself that's some excuse if ever there was one, I've heard it all now! Sure, that's the best bit of them but I suppose beggars can't be choosers. Soggy, tasteless crisps are better than no crisps at all. We have a big crisp factory here in Northern Ireland, I'm guessing it's a very round flat building and it's my dream to visit one day when I would accidentally fall into a big container of fully flavoured crisps and eat them until I boke. I wonder if the factory opens from the top or has a door on the side? I also quite like those cheesy snacks that look like big fat caterpillars. When I'm eating them I feel like I'm doing a bush tucker trial. Mummy and Daddy have tried to suck the flavour of them too but it's more tricky as they tend to melt a bit, leaving even less for me to eat. Ragin! By the way, I happen to know a few dogs who look like big fat caterpillars too, but I'm not naming names. They know exactly who they are and they also know that they would need to be gettin at least as much exercise as I do.

Anyway, I'm off to bed now, to pleasantly dream about Smoky Bacon crisps. I imagine they'd be my favourite because I love bacon and Mummy has never let me eat cheese or onions and so I have no idea what that would taste like.

Night night!'

And so it was that another week of Wee Alfie's life was well and truly under way with Monday drawing to a close as he crawled into his basket. An Irish singer called Bob, 'Get off' or something like that, once sang about how he hated Mondays but it wasn't the case with Wee Alfie, who loved every single day, no matter what day of the week. Of course he didn't understand the meaning of the bit in the song about a silicon chip inside his head being switched to overload. Wee Alfie didn't eat chips, but if that had happened to Wee Alfie then maybe he would have hated Mondays too, just as much as Bob Get off. But no, he had really enjoyed his Monday and knew Tuesday would be just as much fun, if not better, as he closed his eyes and fell sound asleep, breaking wind as suspected at regular intervals as he did so. Tell me more, as the words of the song went. You are about to be told more, do not fear, you've only heard about the first day of seven.

Tuesday

Wee Alfie woke up on this not so fine Tuesday morning and he didn't exactly feel excited about the prospect of a wet rotten oul day. He always says that rainy days mess up his lovely coat and makes it go all curly. Houl your wishst, Wee Alfie couldn't get away with that one cos he has curly hair anyway, whether it's bucketin or sunny. He opened just the one eye as his Daddy staggered into the kitchen, still half asleep so probably with only one eye open too. He hoped Daddy would forget all about letting him out but sadly it wasn't to be. He, Daddy not Wee Alfie, held his cup of coffee in one hand and the key to the back door in the other. Wee Alfie didn't look as keen as usual, in fact he looked downright miserable at the very thought, although it's fair to say he does have that sort of face that looks miserable even when he's happy.

Out he would go and back he would return only to be dropped into a sink of luke warm water followed by a paw-drying session from Mummy. He's got bad feet you see and they require quite a bit of pampering. She always told him off for being a naughty boy, bringing so much mud and gutters into the house while she rubbed his feet clean with a filthy towel, never thinking for one moment it wasn't actually his fault. What did she expect him to do...hover over the garden? Wee Alfie hated it as much as Mummy did, so there was no need for harsh words, take a chill pill Mummy, life's too short.

The kitchen door opened with a creak and the wind blew in, completely uninvited. Daddy frowned and Wee Alfie groaned, neither fancied the day that lay ahead. The crafty doggie pretended he had a bad leg and hobbled to the door before thinking the better of it. A dodgy leg would have meant a trip to the local vet and Wee Alfie was never fond of that scary journey. His master was just about to look at the possibly damaged paw when Alfie saw sense and disappeared out of the kitchen door into the garden. He would have regretted the not so smart move.

Alfie had experienced some truly frightening visits to the vet, some that humans have never have had to go through since the 17th Century, quite possibly when Mummy and Daddy were born according to cheeky Alfie. No, it wasn't his favourite place by any means what with the possibilities and the yapping animals in the waiting room, snarling at each other with gay abandon. Definitely not as well behaved as Wee Alfie cos he's a very good boy...mostly. He once went in all intact and came out with a couple of things missing, ah the cruelty of vets. How would they like it?

He remembered how, on one occasion, he had to sit and wait beside a snake with a toothache or whatever, for a wee while at least, until he climbed up the nearest lampshade in total fear of the thing that looked like a gyrating draught excluder. No, a trip to the vet wasn't for him so he chose the early morning downpour and soaking instead. His wounded paw had miraculously mended.

He was once told the story of how his dear oul Granda took his own dog to the vet years ago and the poor animal had to have one of those big plastic collars put round his neck to stop him licking the wound from the operation. When he got home Wee Alfie's Granda dangled his dog from the living-room ceiling because the plastic thing they put around the dog's neck was much better than the lampshade in the living-room. Believe that one at your peril. Granda had lots of stories like that one.

The rain had brought so many new smells and his nose twitched away ninety to the dozen, like a hamster. Why do hamsters do that? Why don't they just have a good oul blow into a hanky like the rest of us and sort it out? It can't always be a sinus problem, more an annoying habit. Wee Alfie had always been jealous of hamsters, a ridiculous feeling of resentment really. They may be a family pet like him but, in the reasoning mind of Wee Alfie at least, they don't get slung out in the rain first thing in the morning do they? There was nothing to be jealous about though but that didn't stop Wee Alfie endlessly goin on about it. They spend all their time in a cage and relieve themselves on strips of old newspaper in a most undignified way…dorty bruts. There was nothing whatsoever to be jealous about. Exercise? They have nothing more than a stupid wheel that must send them round the bend, their own tiny version of that big circular thing in Belfast at Funderland. I think there's one in England too called the London Eye, not that it looks anything like an eye unless you have a serious eyesight problem, making your eyeball spin madly round and round and it would probably make you boke too.

He looked to his left, a little jumpily until he realised it was just the raindrops dripping onto the path and not beasties attacking from up above. Certain things always got on his wick, pigeons for instance. Now, those things may not seem too scary to the likes of humans but a pigeon, fully fed, is half the size of Wee Alfie. Imagine something that size swooping down on you and you will realise why he didn't trust them, a fact that ties in nicely with the next few hours of this particular Tuesday.

Despite the rain, Mummy and Daddy had decided to sling Wee Alfie in the back of the car and take him to the seaside. Now there's nothing he likes more than being let loose on a beach, the wind in his fur and his ears flapping around like a windmill as he races for miles and miles. This day the trip would be different. He dug away at the sand, just as Mummy had taught him, before adding some other contents to make the smelliest sandcastle for miles.

'I just love going to the beach, into the cage in the boot, for my protection says Mummy but in my opinion, she just can't be bothered nursing me. There's no room on her knee anyway with all the bags of sweets for the journey, most of which she's ate before we've even got out of our village. There's loads of gorgeous beaches in Ireland and I think I may well have peed on them all. One of my favourites is called Inchadoney in County Cork. That's away down the bottom of Ireland and it takes at least three and a quarter weeks to get there, or it certainly seems it anyway. The journey is sooooo long and sooooo boring, a bit like Daytime TV that you heard about yesterday, but it's definitely worth it. I can't even play spot the yellow car on the way cos I can't see a thing apart from the back of their heads. The only time I was actually able to play spot the yellow car I thought I'd won until Daddy told me it was a banana in the fruit bowl. Darn it anyway, I never win nothin!

I really LOVE the beach though and I'm always goin on about it, so much so that Mummy says;

'Alfie are you working for the tourist board?'. She's a geg isn't she?

As soon as my paws hit the sand, oh boy, I go clean buck mad and the poo bags have to come out straight away. I don't really have to go but force myself because it means Daddy has to carry the contents around all day until we find a bin. It gives me a bit of a laugh anyway, especially if he gets stung by a wasp. He really doesn't like having to do that but hey, that's what you've gotta do when you have a dog. If Mummy ever had to go too, it would put him clean over the edge. Imagine having to carry that about. He'd need to hire a crane and a skip. Then I'm off like a bullet again chasing the birds (the feathered and the four-legged kind too).

The first dip in the sea is always a bit of a shock to the system and even with only two steps in, with my wee legs I'm in it up to my oxters. Mummy and Daddy paddle on out trying to coax me to go with them but I haven't forgot the last time when a great big wave pulled me clean off my feet and I floated off in the opposite direction so far that I saw the white cliffs of America. Oh how Mummy and Daddy laughed...really funny, NOT.

Ach well, at least I can have a pee when I'm in the water without the fear of raising the sea level, not like them, well I hope not anyway and I'm sure you do too. Whatever next?

He hadn't been on the beach for more than half an hour when the place became invaded by a flock of seagulls (not the band, the birds). Now if you think pigeons can scare the life out of him, just imagine how he felt about taking on a bunch of even bigger, hungry seagulls with nasty tempers. Now they have serious attitude problems, that's why no-one keeps them as pets.

They reckon that seagulls fly inland when it rains. What a load of rubbish. It WAS raining and the nasty white beasts were quite happy staying at the water's edge and weren't going anywhere any time soon. Wee Alfie reckoned that if seagulls were that bothered about rain then God would have given them umbrellas. Why do seagulls always have great big miserable gubs on them? You never see a happy one. Maybe there aren't any happy ones, which would explain everything.

I HATE them seagulls, looking down their beaks at me with their beady eyes and their big stupid orange flippers on their feet, they think they are something. I'll show them, if I could only catch one that is. I spend loads of time galloping up and down the beach after them but I'm not as stupid as that dog on the telly the other week. He swam after them and he had to be rescued by the lifeboat dear knows how many times. They should have just let carry on swimming so far he ended up on another channel. I think he just did it to get on the telly, bit drastic if you ask me. I have to admit though, there's something I LOVE about seagulls and that is, their poo. They do bucket loads of it and it's really really smelly so just perfect for rolling in. Nothing I like more than being plastered in seagull poo from head to toe. Mummy and Daddy go absolutely mental when I do that and I don't really know why. It's either that they're ragin that they didn't see it before me so that they could have had a good oul roll about in it or the fact that they now have to take me back down to the sea to wash me. I think maybe it's the latter but to be honest seagull poo smells an awful lot nicer than the perfume and aftershave they wear. Someday I WILL catch my first seagull, sure I can always dream.

As his paws splashed about in the sea he happily bounced up and down more than usual as the water tickled his belly. He looked more than happy as he ran along, completely unaware of half a dozen of them seagulls that were following behind him like balloons on strings. It was like a scene from an Alfred Peacock film, or whatever you call him. Mummy and Daddy walked slowly towards the small promenade of shops, not even bothering to try and keep up with their energetic pet doggie who had belted off in the other direction. Wee Alfie slowed down and looked upwards towards the sky as he suddenly realised the enemy overhead. He barked and the rampant seagulls squawked, he barked louder and the seagulls squawked louder. He wasn't going to win that competition, never in a million doggie years.

He called out to his Mummy and Daddy but they couldn't hear him over the noise of the wild birds so they just kept on headin towards the friendly wee shop that sold cups of tea, mouth-watering cakes, sandwiches and other goodies. They sat and took in the beautiful view across the sea as they slurped and nibbled, not realising how fed up Wee Alfie had become with all that was going on.

By the time Wee Alfie made it back to their sides and to safety from the marauding birds they had both settled down, each tucking into a big wholesome home-made sausage roll. Wee Alfie sat down, slabbers tripping him, like all well-mannered dogs do in the hope of getting a piece of the tasty treat. His tail wagged and his head cocked over lovingly to the left in expectation. This particular pose had always worked before and he couldn't have looked sweeter if he'd tried, but under his breath he was demanding food in no uncertain manner. Daddy tossed a small piece into the air assuming Wee Alfie would jump up and catch it in his mouth before it hit the ground. He leapt up like a salmon from a river but that flippin seagull beat him to it, smacking him in the gub with his wing. Wee Alfie let out an almighty yelp and ran around in a huge circle for no apparent reason as the winged-beast flew off with a piece of sausage roll, half the size of its head.

Mummy laughed her head off, not really necessary it had to be said, and began singing Feed The Birds from Mary Poppins. It wasn't a great song and it wasn't sung too well either. Wee Alfie gave a look of despair as did Daddy, neither being that overly impressed by the sound of a strangled cat.

Sometimes I don't know why I bother begging cos them two greedy hallions wouldn't give you a bite. I've tried my best wee face, my best sitting up and beg (very like a meerkat), my gentle nudge on the leg followed by a strong pull on the bottom of the trousers, my pathetic cry and wimper sequence and finally some loud barking. All of which have had no effect except for me getting barged. What is the point of spending hour upon hour trying to teach me to, give my paw, roll over, sit, lie down, beg etc when you're not going to use it. Just like you humans learning algebra and Latin...what's the point? How do you order a fish supper in Latin anyway? I took ages to learn all them commands, not because I'm stupid, oh no. I pretended to take ages cos every time they tried to show me they had to give me another treat, so no point in learning too quickly! I'm not as slow as I walk easy. Mummy says no more treats for the foreseeable cos I'm getting too fat (pot and kettle) and that I need to watch what I eat. I DO watch what I eat. And then I eat it. Simple! What's the problem?

The trip to the seaside over, Wee Alfie was glad to be back home safe and sound, albeit a bit sandy round the nether regions. It has to be said he'd enjoyed the trip to the coast until the seagull incident but the scary ending was all he could think about as he settled into his basket for a quick doze before his dinner. He snored and twitched as he re-lived the moment. He loved the sea air and the wind rushing through his hair and he loved to run as fast as his tiny paws would carry him, but enough was enough. He loved sausage rolls more but he'd had to go without. Get the violins out.

He closed his eyes for a good hour or more until the sound of Daddy tapping the dog bowl returned him to his senses. His dinner was ready and this time he didn't have to jump in the air for his grub when he heard the clanging sound. He rose from his basket, had a wee stretch and trotted across before getting stuck in to his dinner, his dinner and nobody else's.

Mummy and Daddy settled down to listen to a few albums of folk music, but Wee Alfie wasn't interested in the slightest. Many of the songs told of beautiful parts of both Northern and Southern Ireland, wonderful vocal landscapes of mountains, loughs and bays, the very places where them seagulls flew around in the sky. He imagined them all swooping down on him like fighter planes in The Second World War and he didn't fancy the idea one little bit, thank you very much. Mummy and Daddy joined in each chorus (very badly) and it only made matters worse.

Please oh please, make them stop! If I hear them sing another diddle-de-dee song and even worse, another banjo solo, I think I'll go mental. Two questions for you...Who in the name of goodness invented the banjo and are where can I possibly buy earplugs for dogs? If anybody would know where to get the earplugs it would be Mummy, with all her expertise in buying stuff on Ebay. I must ask her when she can actually hear me over all that racket. Come to think of it she has some, I know that because when we're away in the van she can't stick me and Daddy snoring...couldn't be any worse than what she's listening to now. They have me trailed to every music festival they can find. I was only 4 months old when I went to my first one in Westport, County Mayo. I must admit, I really enjoyed myself and even though Mummy and Daddy were performing at it, I got considerably more attention than them. They were rippin but lets face it, I'm so much cuter. I even went to their gig in Matt Molloy's and slept upside down on the stage throughout the whole thing. I was knackered after a long day on Bertra Strand chasing them seagulls..still didn't catch one.

It was time for the final wee before bed and Wee Alfie edged out of the kitchen door, looking up to the sky in case any white villains were still around. The coast was clear, the opposite to what he had witnessed earlier, but he still felt a little uncertain even though he lived in the country and there weren't any seagulls there...but you never know, they could have followed him home. He cocked his leg as quickly as he could and he'd barely finished his business before running back into the safety of the house. There were no smells to investigate, no creepy crawlies to stare out, just a three-quarter finished wee and back indoors, leaving a glistening trail in the moonlight. It all seemed like something poetry was made of.

Tuesday had come to an end and Wee Alfie was certain to sleep well as he forgot all about those wicked birds and looked forward to a far more peaceful Wednesday. He rolled onto his back gave a few sighs of pleasure and he was off into dreamland.

Well, what a funny oul day that was. I can go to bed with a full belly, although it could've been fuller if I had got myself a bit of that sausage roll, tired out after all the fear and excitement. I wonder where they'll take me tomorrow? It'll probably be somewhere great because we're having to write about it in this book, so it wouldn't be a very interesting read for you if it was somewhere boring, would it?

I hope I meet up with my girlfriend Wee Judy very soon to tell her about all my shenanigans. Maybe I could find some of that seagull poo to splash on before we meet up. She'd be well impressed that I'd made such an effort, the stinkier the better, that's what I reckon. Maybe I'll bring her a sausage roll too. Night night Wee Judy, wherever you are. I hope you are dreaming about me.

Wednesday

On this weird Wednesday morning Wee Alfie found himself upside down when he woke up, his legs akimbo in the air like a beaten boxer, the fighter not the dog. He couldn't work out why and that was hardly surprising as there was no real reason at all why this had happened, so there was absolutely nothing for him to work out really.

The noise of his Mummy walking into the kitchen and stubbing her toe on the cupboard door scared the livin daylights clean out of him and forced his eyes to open quicker than expected. All he could see was the ceiling, oh and a lightbulb dangling down from it. For a minute he hadn't the foggiest notion where he was. The white ceiling that filled his eyes was all he could see and he thought he'd been caught in a snowstorm, a violent snowstorm. There was no way in this world he was going out in that kind of weather and so he closed his eyes and tried to go back to sleep, but it just didn't work.

Daddy had run down the hall like a man possessed when he'd heard Mummy screaming her head off as Wee Alfie tried to work out where the winter blizzard had come from.

'Is it broken?' Wee Alfie heard the worried man ask his gurnin wife.

Wee Alfie re-opened his right eye and looked at the kitchen cupboard. It wasn't broke, wasn't even scratched, so what was all the fuss about, she'd need to wind her neck in, he thought. The kitchen units were made from sturdier stuff than that and would be nearly impossible to damage should a toe scrape across them. Thankfully it must have been a false alarm but it was still a very annoying start to his Wednesday.

The reluctant doggie was lifted from his basket by a limping, sobbing and snattery Mummy for his regulation walkie first thing. By the time he reached the kitchen door his fur was soaking and his ears were close to perforation because the tears were trippin her and her constant wailin was going right through him. She turned the key, the door creaked open and Wee Alfie was at the mercy of the snowstorm he thought had happened during the night when he first woke up.

Just imagine his surprise when he looked around the garden and there was a lovely blue sky and not a single snowflake to be seen anywhere. Wee Alfie looked confused, very confused, he had every right to be confused. He tried to scratch his head but the last time he did an irritated flea went for him. He looked back at the kitchen and then at the garden. He looked around the garden and then back to the kitchen. It was at that moment, Wee Alfie came to the conclusion that Northern Ireland had the best snow-plough drivers in the whole wide world.

If the truth be told, I'm a wee bit disappointed that it's not snowing cos I LOVE the snow. The first time I ever clapped eyes on any, Mummy opened the back door and I couldn't believe what I was seeing. Everything was all white and I thought to myself 'has somebody had the bleach out when I was in my kipper?' I was a wee bit nervous about tramping about in it but Mummy gently coaxed me with her foot on my rear end, making me slide across the kitchen tiles on my belly trying desperately to find something to dig my nails into. But when I did eventually and unwillingly go out, oh boy, the feeling of that freezing cold snow on the paws, sent me tearing off in circles round the garden. I had to keep running to stay warm cos it would've foundered ya. The more I ran, the more flakes of the sticky snow stuck to me. By the time I was ready to go in again I was about four sizes bigger than I was when I first went out. Mummy had to put me in the sink again to thaw out. I'm never out of that sink, I must have the cleanest doggie under carriage in Ireland. I'm surprised she doesn't sling me in with the washing-up sometimes. Owww, imagine sitting on a knife and fork. Snow is amazing though and best of all, you can eat it, as long as it's not yellow, for some reason, although I personally think it tastes nicer.

A locka years ago we were snowed in and they couldn't get the car out. So, Daddy said we would have to go on a bit of a hiking expedition to the village shop for essentials, whatever they may be apart from Bonios, that's what I call essentials anyway. Mummy and Daddy piled on layer upon layer of clothes and we were well happed up. They even made me put a coat on, the one with the really big collar that makes me look like Elvis. I ask you, how can just a collar make you look like a loaf of brown bread. Houl on a minute, that might be Hovis I'm thinking of. Anyway, I said I didn't want to wear it in case I met Wee Judy, but when I saw the look on Mummy's bake, on it went. Anything for a quiet life.

So off we went on a journey that usually takes around five minutes in the car. Four hours later and after a full repertoire of moaning was covered and ignored by myself, we were at the shop. They tied me up outside in my Elvis coat and I was in the middle of a rendition of 'Hound Dog' when out they came with the 'essentials'. This turned out to be four bars of chocolate and a six pack of cheese and onion crisps. No doubt I'll be getting some of those later with the flavour sucked off them. Grateful for small mercies, that's me.'

He sniffed the grass, it wasn't even damp let alone sodden and a not a single snowflake to be seen. Then he trotted along the bone-dry path that should have been covered in ice. There was definitely no ice. It all made Wee Alfie remember the story his Granda had told him of how, many years ago, the winters were so cold that the oul crater had to sit on a radiator so his wee would thaw out. Imagine that. According to him, other dogs were weeing against lampposts and icicles were forming before their cocked legs were back on the ground. Unbelievable!

Wee Alfie realised how lucky he was as he ran around the garden on this Wednesday morning that quickly changed from hectic to normal, well as normal as things could be with his Mummy limping around the place with a broken toe. Times were much harder for dogs all them years ago when, according to Granda, they used to work down the mines, shifting tons of coal or pulled piles of peat along miles of forest paths. It really was a dog's life way back then.

Wee Alfie barked a good morning to his girlfriend Wee Judy but there was no reply. Maybe she wasn't up yet. He dreamed of waking up one morning with a gorgeous girl by his side until he came to his senses and realised his basket wasn't big enough for two dogs. No way was he sharing it with anybody, no matter how much he thought of her.

Despite the odd start it had turned into a beautiful day. It was crisp. That didn't mean the air stank of cheese and onion, it just meant that there was a slight nip in the air which gave Wee Alfie a cold and somewhat snattery nose. It certainly woke him up anyway and he trotted back in like a new dog, so to speak.

Wee Alfie was suddenly left home alone as Daddy had decided to set off for the hospital with Mummy moaning and groaning in the back of the car. She really was taking the biscuit and making a meal of the incident with the kitchen cupboard. She'd banged her toe for heaven's sake, not fell off the side of a mountain or been ate alive by sharks. She was such a head the ball. However, it gave Wee Alfie a chance to rest quietly without any interruption. Normally that's exactly what he would have done, but this morning he thought he would do something far more exciting.

He wasn't that tired and so he took a wee stroll round the house, checking things out, strange things he'd never noticed before or ever been allowed to notice before. He'd entered the out of bounds world. In the music room, for instance, he jumped onto the piano, usually forbidden, and he laughed his head off as the notes rang out from underneath his paws. The notes were in no particular order and it sounded awful, a bit like modern jazz. From the piano he made his way to where Daddy's guitar leaned against the wall. He rubbed his ear across the strings and another desperate sound rang out, just like it did when Daddy tried to play it. It all made sense. Daddy played the guitar with his ear while Mummy walked across the piano when she had ten perfectly healthy toes, before one had painfully gone to the piggy market, or the hospital at least. Alfie had a good oul laugh to himself once more as he made his way back to the kitchen, his eyes gazing everywhere in search of new things.

He knew he'd done something very naughty when he leapt up onto the kitchen table to see if any titbits had been left before the trip to A&E. Have you ever seen a dog trying to unzip a banana? Forget it. He did find his bag of biscuits though and picked out his favourite pink ones before he neatly closed the top. He was really enjoying his journey to Aladdin's cave when he suddenly heard the car pull up outside the house, making him gallop to his basket, lie down and close his eyes. He even pretended to snore, not easy for a dog who doesn't really mean it.

Mummy limped in wearing a shoe on one foot and a huge white sock on the other. For goodness sake she'd only hurt her toe, not gone wandering off into a blizzard with Captain Scott and caught frostbite. Drama queen was no name for it thought Wee Alfie. He treads on stinging nettles and thistles in his bare paws, walks on jagged pieces of rock and tree branches, but you wouldn't catch him going for an Oscar winning performance like that. It wasn't surprising when he seemed so unimpressed.

Mummy did some extreme hobbling into the living room and Wee Alfie followed, thinking it was the very least he could do. She plonked down with a thud, sighed deeply and stuck her damaged foot on the coffee table. Wee Alfie tried to do the same but immediately fell over. His tumble cheered Mummy up no end and she patted him on the head, fully aware at least he'd made the effort.

The next three and a half hours were spent slabberin on her mobile to relations, friends and even people she didn't know or like, telling them all how lucky she was to be alive, it was a miracle! It meant the afternoon walk had been cancelled, causing a ragin Wee Alfie to curse his luck as he'd had a funny feeling all morning he would meet up with Wee Judy that afternoon. Sadly, it wasn't to be. They say every dog has its day, but this day wasn't it and no such day for our wee fella. Thank goodness he hadn't bothered to buy a lottery ticket as no numbers would have come up, unlike his Mummy who acted as though her own number was well and truly up.

So, all in all, it wasn't the most energetic of Wednesdays for Wee Alfie, but the day did end on a high note. Daddy cooked the dinner while Mummy took it easy on the settee, and boy oh boy, what a dinner he cooked. The kitchen smelt gorgeous and the slabbers were trippin Wee Alfie as a great big roast leg of pork was pulled from the oven along with a pile of yummy roast potatoes. Wee Alfie couldn't believe his luck when Mummy decided a bowl of soup would be safer for her stomach considering she was still in a state of shock from the broken toe.

They were going to have the dinner on their knees in the living room so Daddy gave a deep sigh as he returned hers to the kitchen and took a tin of soup from the cupboard. Wee Alfie's adding up had never been his strong point but it wasn't too difficult even for him to realise there were two stonkin great roast dinners and only one would be ate. He realised after giving it some thought that there would be one left over. Such a clever boy.

He never took his eyes off Daddy for one second as he heated up the soup and buttered a couple of slices of white pan loaf, the most boring bread that had ever been buttered. He cocked his head in such a loveable way, knowing full well that this was a chance he couldn't let slip from his paws, a full roast dinner that would otherwise be slung in the bin. Gravy bones were one thing but real slurpy, tasty gravy was something else altogether. Wee Alfie's tail began to wag off him like a windscreen wiper in a storm at the very thought of it, but Daddy saw that as a signal that he needed to go out into the garden as a matter of urgency. Oh how wrong Daddy was. The last thing Wee Alfie wanted was to leave that roast dinner, even for one moment. He wanted to get his chops around that roast pork, end of. It wasn't every day Mummy broke her toe and got an Equity card all in one go. He saw the lovely dinner as a form of celebration.

The back door was unlocked and with not exactly the gentlest of shoves Wee Alfie found himself out on his backside, skidding along the grass like some wound-up toy. His Daddy had indeed misunderstood the tail wagging as expected and it seemed Wee Alfie's plan had backfired.

It turned out to be the quickest walk he had ever taken. He didn't visit a single tree or smell a single smell. He was out one second and the next he was back in the kitchen at his Daddy's feet. He looked all around, saw a plate with a mountain of a roast dinner and a bowl of soup that was about to make it's way to the living room where the invalid sat with one leg akimbo. There was no second roast dinner anywhere to be seen.

Mummy and Daddy sat down beside each other on the settee enjoying their dinner, although their meals were chalk and cheese in terms of content. Wee Alfie lay on the carpet by their four legs and nineteen fit toes as they tucked into their Wednesday evening dinner. Alfie kept looking up longingly but without much luck. He thought he would have a chance to lick Daddy's plate clean, minimum, but no joy.

Mummy called it a day and no-one could have blamed her as it had been many hours of great pain and even greater acting, so she'd had enough. It seemed to take her an eternity to get to the bedroom so perhaps another award was on its way. Daddy returned with a smile on his face, the first one of the day, and he instructed Wee Alfie to follow him into the kitchen. The doggie's hopes rose with his body and he trotted in.

'I have something very special for you,' Daddy told him. Oh, such excitement, Wee Alfie had never been allowed to lick a dinner plate before, it made him feel quite the boyo.

'Here you are, Wee Alfie, get stuck into this.'

Wee Alfie looked up. No, it wasn't the scrapins from the finished dinner plate after all. Out Daddy went to the fridge and pulled out a FULL roast dinner, as high as Wee Alfie's body.

Alfie was thinking, does he expect me to eat this or climb it? There was everything on there, from roast pork to roast potatoes, lashings of thick, brown gravy and various yucky vegetables that he wasn't fussed on and could spit out on the mat later. It was amazing and Wee Alfie's tail wagged so much it nearly fell clean off.

'Don't tell Mummy sure you won't?,' Daddy told him. Wee Alfie scuffed his paw on the floor in reply. It was a deal.

Wee Alfie had never eaten so much in his whole life, far more than was good for his health, but sure what of it, a wee treat every now and again wouldn't do him a button of harm. He was full to burstin, so much so that if he'd gone out into the garden and stood on a hedgehog he would have exploded like a party balloon. Having said that, Daddy made sure his wee pet, if you'll pardon the pun, went out for a darn good emptying before matters were closed for the day, so off he slowly went. He couldn't run, he was so full of dinner, he could barely waddle, but he reached the end of the garden and added some more compost to the heap without ceremony. He wasn't fond of gardening but he liked to do his bit just the same. Clever gardeners, who know what they're talking about, say that manure is good for the garden and as Wee Alfie says, someone has to do it. What he doesn't understand is if manure is good for growing things then why don't people grow vegetables in the toilet?

Wednesday drew to a close, a very strange Wednesday indeed, it has to be said. Wednesday is often the most boring day of the week but not on this occasion. It was strange, end of. Everything is a little bit strange in the life of Wee Alfie. Wouldn't you agree?

Thursday

How time flies, three days have already disappeared this week and sure it's Thursday already, would you believe it? It should be the same oul routine every day for Wee Alfie, the same as it is for other dogs, but he is definitely no ordinary dog. Something seems to happen to him every single day that makes him very special and this Thursday would be no exception. Today, Wee Alfie is hoping it's going to be a very special day indeed.

It turns out that his Mummy had been on the phone to Wee Judy's Mummy, Brenda, and they've planned a joint walk around the park with their two doggies. Why is that so special you may well ask? In case you didn't already know, Wee Alfie is in big love with Wee Judy ever since the very first day they met. They did the usual muckin about and sniffin each-other but there was something a whole lot more between them, something that only other dogs could understand.

The day normally begins with a wee quick dander round the garden as you have probably gathered from the previous three days, followed by a longer walkies in the afternoon, but this particular Thursday it would be oh so different. There would be no early-morning relief in the back garden, no, not today. It would be a delightful longer walk first thing as Mummy and Brenda had stuff to do in the afternoon. Wee Alfie just couldn't wait. The early morning smells would be loads more exciting than normal and the views would be stunning, in more ways than one. The last exciting Thursday that Wee Alfie could remember was when he happened to meet up with Seamus the Sheepdog, a passing acquaintance. He was getting some exercise ready for a sheepdog trial and Wee Alfie felt so sorry for him, whatever he had done. It must have been a worrying time for poor Seamus getting ready to stand in court and plead his innocence and yet he seemed to put all his worries behind him when he met up with Wee Alfie and had a bit of a romp. Wee Alfie wished him luck and hoped they would meet up again in a few years when Seamus, if found guilty of course, was released.

Since she met Wee Alfie, Wee Judy hasn't let another dog go next nor near her, such is her affection for Wee Alfie, but today is the very first time they are officially 'steppin out' together. You can imagine how busy he's been, licking his fur like nobody's business and making sure his curls are bouncy and in top notch condition. One minute he's beside himself with excitement and the next he's scared stiff at the thought of his first ever date. Luckily, Wee Judy has been equally excited and determined to look as stunningly beautiful as she could possibly be. Yes, it was to be a very special day for the two of them.

'Mummy and Daddy have known each other for about 6 million years and are still together and stuck with each-other for eternity. That super-glue is amazing stuff. Mummy says that if she had killed Daddy, she'd be out of prison by now and livin it up but Daddy says she'd be lost without him. He's probably right because her sense of direction is shocking. She needs a satnav to go to the bathroom. They met on a night out with some friends and Mummy said that she liked Daddy then because he made her laugh...well your not laughin now Mummy are ya? And you only have yourself to blame for that one. So their first date was in a restaurant

and Daddy ordered a great big steak. He ate all the spuds and veg first and then around the edges of the steak until he had a juicy tasty wee square of meat left to savour. The best bit by all accounts. Then Mummy said 'Oh look, there's your next door neighbour comin in', so when Daddy looked round, Mummy stole and ATE his last bit of steak. He was RAGIN let me tell ya but unbelievably still married her, so I have absolutely no sympathy for him.

Mummy says that she wouldn't let him be in the wedding photos in case people felt too sorry for her and when she cut the wedding cake she found a file hidden in the top layer to help her escape. As my dear oul granny once said, you make your dog bed and you just have to lie in it.

Maybe I could take Wee Judy to that posh restaurant sometime. She's not getting steak though, it's too dear. I'm not made of money, she can have a gravy bone, like it or lump it.'

Wee Alfie waited at the kitchen door for ages before his Mummy was ready to leave. He had to be really patient but was pacing the floor cos he daren't be late in case Brenda went off to the park with Wee Judy on her own. What if Wee Judy thought that Wee Alfie wasn't interested? Of course he was interested, she was gorgeous. He kept looking at himself in the glass of the kitchen door, adjusting any sticky-up hairs on his ears and around his eyes, shaking with anticipation. He looked very fanciable (even though he said so himself) and was ready for action. He had no need to worry.

He set off with his tail sticking straight up like a poker and trotting like a horse in a dressage competition. He was a man on a mission.

So what about Wee Judy? Who is she, what breed and what does she look like? For starters, she's really wee, she has to be small really because Wee Alfie isn't exactly a giant of an animal. She is pure white unless she has been rolling in the gutters or things which are far more undesirable. She's one of them Highland Terrier's, a very strange name for such a small dog. Why would such a low-slung dog want to live on high land? Being a Highland Terrier you'd think that she would bark with a Scottish accent, maybe she does, only Alfie could possibly know the answer to that one, but sadly he hasn't the foggiest idea what a Scottish accent is having never been to Scotland in his entire life.

Whichever way you look at it Wee Judy is an absolute cracker, which caused great concern for Wee Alfie who thought this meant she could only be pulled at Christmas and sure that was months away. He couldn't possibly wait that long. Once again, he had no need to worry.

When they reached the park Brenda was already waiting there with the gorgeous Wee Judy. The two tails nearly wagged clean off them and they almost choked, leads pulling tighter and tighter as they got nearer and nearer. Wee Alfie's nails were nearly ground down to the quick on the tarmac as he tried desperately to get to his girlfriend. They couldn't take their eyes off each other as the two Mummys slabbered on and on and on about nothing in particular, just like Mummys do. All they wanted was to be set free so as they could race off as fast as their tiny wee legs would carry them. Wee Judy whined with sheer excitement and frustration, it was a delightful yet soft whine to remind Brenda she wanted to be let off the lead. However, she didn't want to overdo the whining as she was trying to play hard to get…treat them mean and keep them keen she thought to herself. Clever Wee Judy. Brenda didn't seem to take any notice as she carried on yapping, ninety to the dozen, about the weather, noisy neighbours and something she'd bought online, along with what they'd watched on the telly the night before. Wee Alfie was having none of it, so he gave off the loudest bark he could muster scaring the livin daylights out of both Mummys making them stop talking and look down in surprise. He had his head cocked to one side and his tail dragged on the floor racin from east to west and back again at a rate of knots. Then the moment came, the golden moment, the kind they show at the start of a romantic film.

The two of them galloped off like greyhounds and in a few short moments they were just tiny specs in the distance, enjoying their first real moment together, on their own, as a couple. Mummy and Brenda didn't have a clue where they had gone or what they would be doing as their disappearance hadn't stopped the slabberin, this time talking about their favourite dog-groomers. Wee Alfie had only ever been to the dog-groomers for a wee trim, just that sort of thing, but he'd never had his eyebrows plucked, endured a pointless manicure or had his fur platted into a ponytail as if he was off to some high level dog show. Wee Alfie was a proper bloke after all and he was having none of that oul nonsense.

The two dogs ran past the kids play area without a second glance, they weren't interested in swings or roundabouts or sand pits full of coloured, plastic balls for that matter. They sped past the lake to their right too as neither of them fancied diving into the water and wrecking their perfectly groomed hair. Yes, they wouldn't have minded sitting in a Venetian gondola, holding paws and being paddled along while they drank some cockertails, but beyond that they weren't too excited at the thought of water. Wee Alfie didn't fancy swimming in the same stuff that fish weed in, definitely not today anyway. No, all they wanted to do was run and then run further and further with the wind flappin in their ears.

They discovered a great big wild flowerbed at the far end of the park and that was where they rested up, gently sniffing and tail-wagging at each other, away from prying eyes. The smell of the flowers was beautiful and made the moment far more special. It was a moment of sheer pleasure, at least it was until a brute of a bulldog called Buster, (and why so many bulldogs are called Buster is anyone's guess), broke their peace and quiet, galloping towards them like a raging bull, probably hence the name. He took an immediate fancy to Wee Judy, (well why wouldn't he, she's a looker) scaring the wits clean out of Wee Alfie as he did so. Wee Alfie took a few steps back, not wishing to get into a fight with a dog three times his size and one with an anger management problem.

That may well have been the end to their very first date but Wee Judy was having none of that. She gave the gate-crashing beast a nasty nip on the leg that sent him yelping and limping away defeated in David and Goliath fashion. He was last seen chasing a three-legged scrap of a cat with only one ear whose name, against all the odds, was Lucky. You lose Buster the Bulldog, well done to Wee Judy.

She didn't look like she had it in her to be so brutal or aggressive towards another dog, so

Wee Alfie realised he needed to keep on the right side of her if he wasn't to have the same treatment. It wasn't a bad thing to know, although they both doubted they would ever have such disagreements. After all, neither of them had ever seen their Mummys and Daddys argue. Aye right!

It had been an hour and a half of absolute sheer bliss before the time came to return to their Mummys. This was because they could hear the shrieks of high-pitched whistling and calling which would have went right through ya. Yes, oh what a dog gone shame. They wondered how they would meet up again as they couldn't write letters or send texts, so they had to dream up a cunning plan. After all, they both lived in the same road, so they were bound to find a way of getting back together. That's how and why the next plan was hatched.

'I love where we live. It's in the back of beyond, surrounded by loads of trees all of which I have attempted to pee on at various times, depending on my stamina levels. There's cows in the field beside the house and there's nothing I love more than standing at the fence

barking my head off at them. They don't seem too bothered, in fact they call their mates over as well to have a good oul look at me. They're probably thinking, would you look at that wee eejit giving off to US!! Can you imagine?

I often look at cows and think about the first person ever to milk one. What did he think he was doing? Good job he didn't try the same with a bull eh? That would have been a red rag to, oh never mind.

Daddy barbecues great big steaks in the garage cos he doesn't want to offend the cows. Fair enough, it's a rotten way for them to meet their departed friends and relations. He's very thoughtful that way is Daddy. I don't care where he cooks them as long as I get a bit, a great big juicy bit at that. I look at the size of them cows and hope that there's a great big juicy bit of one of them coming my way in the near future. Daddy keeps a close eye on Mummy now when he's eating his steak, especially after what happened on their first date.

They don't like me begging so I have to lie at their feet pretending not to be interested but once I hear the cutlery rattling on the plates, I know they've nearly finished. That's when I can't help myself and up I go like a meerkat just in case they've forgot me. In fairness I usually do get a wee bit but it's nothing compared to what I get at my Granny and Grandas, they have me ruined. Mummy gives off to them cos she's the one who has to pick up the after effects of all the treats the next day in the garden. Thankfully they don't listen to her, in one ear and out the other. I love going to Granny and Grandas house. They also have lovely fluffy carpet for me to roll about on, not like them hard wooden shiny floors in our our house. It looks like I'm at Dundonald Ice Bowl when I'm running down our hall, legs skiddin all over the shop. I've done the splits loads of times. I might enter the Doggie Winter Olympics next year. Yeah, I don't mind beggin, it certainly isn't beneath me, sure look at the size of me, NOTHING is beneath me. I learnt to beg because I've never been given a shillin in my whole life, so it's their fault and not mine I've had to behave like that silly wee child in thon Charles Dickens film. Charles Dickens, now he really could write a powerful song. That's according to my Granda who I'm told has a slight drink problem. Me too, I spill tons of it when I'm slurpin from the bowl. Aye, you try it yourself if you think it's that easy.'

They decided to both bark and beg to go out just as the 10 o'clock news came on the telly, knowing only too well that both owners opened their back doors for the late-night stroll without setting foot in the gardens themselves. This meant both Wee Judy and Wee Alfie could enjoy five or ten minutes of freedom. Can you possibly imagine the excitement as it drew ever closer to ten o'clock? It was like something out of Cinderella what with keeping an eye on the hands going round. Bot Wee Alfie and Wee Judy hoped and prayed their owners wouldn't nod off in their armchairs and forget to let them out. Oh such a tragic end to a wonderful love story that would be. No, the dogs were having none of that and they both knew a few scrapes and scuffles would keep those eyes open.

And so it was that at 10pm, as their owners put on the news headlines, the dogs upped and went into the kitchen and the two doors were opened. It was dark and so Mummy never saw Wee Alfie leap over the fence like a racehorse and head towards Brenda's garden.

There she was, his lovely girlfriend waiting for him and they were beside themselves to be back together again, sniffing and tail-wagging like the clappers.

Brenda had told Wee Judy's Daddy all about Wee Alfie and how well the dogs seemed to get on when let off the lead. Her Daddy wasn't all that impressed as he'd never met Wee Alfie and so he wasn't too sure if he was good enough for his Wee Judy. He wanted to meet Wee Alfie before another joint walk in the park happened. It was hardly surprising as that's what Daddys do when their wee girls attract attention from the boys. Of course he had no need to worry about our wonderful Wee Alfie but sure he didn't know that. He wanted to see things for himself and to that end, he would take Wee Judy on her next trip to the park.

Wee Alfie fell asleep as soon as he got back home, dreaming about his brilliant day with Wee Judy and bringing the perfect Thursday to a close. Goodnight Wee Alfie and goodnight Wee Judy.

Friday

Friday was never Wee Alfie's favourite day when it came to walkies and every Friday was always exactly the same. It was the day before the weekend so it meant a few hours being dragged like a sack of spuds around the shops on his lead. Because he knew this, he always took forever getting out of his basket to start the day, as he wasn't that fussed on going. Even if the sun was splitting the trees in a beautiful clear blue sky he wasn't too fond of the journey and if it was bucketin with rain, well that was a definite no-no. Sometimes he pretended to be feeling a bit poorly by coughing and spluttering, in the hope of being left behind for a snooze, not too much playing up though or Mummy and Daddy would make a swift diversion to the dreaded vet's and that wasn't Wee Alfie's kettle of fish either. It rarely worked and he knew just how far to take the acting. He yawned, stretched and slid out of his basket ready for the journey into town.

He was slung in the back of the car where he sat, bored to tears, not being tall enough, or interested enough as it happens, to look out of the window on the way to the shops. To make matters worse, Wee Alfie wasn't actually allowed in any of the shops, something Wee Alfie will dispute shortly because there was the one exception, and was tied up to various lamp-posts outside various places, just like a horse outside the saloon in a cowboy film. He hated it. He really hated it. It wasn't easy for a dog to be tied to a lamp-post without relieving itself on the pavement, something that never went down too well. Well it did actually, it went down to the kerb like a great big yellow stream in full flow.

Anyway, that was what happened on a Friday morning and this Friday was no different as he prepared himself for the most boring walk of the week.

Judging by the look on the bakes of his Mummy and Daddy they weren't too keen on the Friday shop either. They never spoke a word to each other on the way to the car-park and they nearly took the doors clean off their hinges, slamming them shut as the shopping mission began. They hadn't actually fought the bit out, they just weren't talking and it's difficult to have an argument when nobody's talking.

Wee Alfie jumped off the back seat, out into the street and immediately began swerving around boots and prams, loads of them. It was like being on the bumper cars at Barrys in Portrush, knowing full well that there'd be a crash at some point. The babies in the prams were about the same height as Wee Alfie and he roared and laughed to himself at how the wee ones, equally bored with them plastic things stuffed in their gubs to stop them crying, reeled away in fear as he stared them out with a fearsome look. It was a powerful game Wee Alfie loved to play with the poor little things, showing his teeth and pretending to be aggressive. Yes, aggressive, Wee Alfie who ran away from a fluttering crisp packet. The bold boy considered it a victory if they started to bawl. Naughty Wee Alfie.

The first port of call was the greengrocer's where, Wee Alfie assumed, they sold green groceries. He was never sure though because he never went inside the shop. It's strange to think that poor Wee Alfie has never been in a shop in his whole life and that's probably why he never has any new clothes to wear. Wee Alfie wearing clothes? No, but perhaps he would if he was allowed to have a wee nosy round a clothes shop. Who knows? Can you imagine Wee Alfie in a pair of gutties or a nice denim shirt, he really would look like no goats toe, wouldn't he? No, I suppose you're right.

'Sure what are they thinkin of? I HAVE been into a shop before for heaven's sake! Their head's are away. Mummy took me to Pets at Home on my birthday to buy me a wee pressie and some doggie treats. Well, that was an experience and a half but sadly I'm not allowed back in again and here's why.

I couldn't believe my luck when Mummy said she was taking me into the pet shop, not that I wanted a pet of my own I should say. She walked me round and round the car park to make sure I was empty before we went in. Oh boy!!! The smells and sounds that hit me as I went through that door were off the scale. I didn't know where to look first.

There were so many toys to choose from, squeaky, fluffy, bouncy, stretchy, you name it and they had it, tempting me right before my eyes. I got a big chicken with rope legs and an annoying squeaky belly, not a real one I hasten to add but a rubber one. Daddy's just loved it..NOT! Then it was off to the clothing department to try on harnesses and jumpers. Didn't enjoy that much, standing in the aisle in my all together and getting my head stuck in the neck of a jumper. One of the shop assistants had to help Mummy get it wrenched off me, such a palaver or 'pullover' as it was. The electricity and static in my fur could have powered a whole housing estate for at least a year. I HATE them jumpers.

I could feel a pee coming on because all I could smell was those other dogs who'd been in and it's only natural that I'd have to mark my territory too. But every time I attempted to lift the oul leg Mummy had the neck pulled off me.

'No Alfie' she'd shout.

I just don't get it, she let me pee all over the place before we went in, so why not now? Well I was just about to find out when momentarily Mummy got distracted and I was able to do a great big flood all over the hamster cage which left them with a rather warm yellowy swimming pool in the middle of their enclosure. Oh dear, Mummy was mortified and looked around to check if anyone had seen. I was quickly marched out of the premises and told in no uncertain terms that I would never set paws in that place again. Mummy had been showed up to the hilt. So, no more Pets at Home for me and worst of all, no more mini bones (that's the only place you can get them). Maybe if I got my hair done a different colour I could sneak back in unrecognised? I'm a bit worried about them hamsters too.'

The Friday morning trip to the shops took a couple of long boring hours laced with Mummy and Daddy's stress and he couldn't wait to get back home to the safety of his basket while they unloaded the bulging shopping bags into the cupboards. He knew which cupboard they kept his tins of food and biscuits in and he wagged his tail a wee bit when he saw the shelf being loaded up with doggie goodies. There was a box of his favourite gravy bones and various tins of meat to get him through the week. Perhaps, if he was a good boy, they would fire a treat his way if he grabbed their attention and so, with that in mind, he jumped up onto Daddy's knee as he sat at the kitchen table slurpin at a cup of coffee. He licked Daddy's face causing him to dribble out a mouthful of coffee all down the front of his shirt. Daddy was rippin. Well, Wee Alfie, that idea was a bit of a disaster wasn't it? He jumped down, climbed back into his basket and fell asleep, even though it was still only early afternoon. Sadly, that was Wee Alfie's walk for the day over and done with and he had hated every single step. It was nothing like the Thursday romp in the park and he hoped the walk the next day would be a bit more exciting too.

Mummy spent most of the afternoon mucking around on social media, posting up pictures and videos of Wee Alfie. It made her feel dead proud even though Wee Alfie himself thought the pictures didn't really do him justice. They never seemed to catch his good side.

'Mummy and Daddy are never off the social media, they're completely obsessed with it. They even send each other messages when they're in the same room. Can you believe it? It's ruining the art of conversation and that's one of the main reasons why I started talking. Well

somebody has to in this house and if it isn't them two, it's me.

Mummy was told in no uncertain terms to get a pair of earphones because she was looking at stuff on YouTube while Daddy was trying to watch the telly and he lost the plot. So now with the earphones in, she tries to sing along completely out of tune like an oul wailin cat and talks twenty times louder than normal. Even without the twenty times more, it's loud enough as it is. It was definitely better before the earphones if you ask me, still too loud but I had learnt how to handle it by closing my ears.'

The one picture he really wanted to see was that of him and his girlfriend Wee Judy, paw in paw, strolling through the park, a far cry from the disastrous Friday morning shopping expedition he'd just experienced. That would have been a lovely picture as far as he was concerned. As Wee Alfie slept he imagined her in a stunning white, frilly, wedding coat and a collar laced in rose petals. Oh yes, Wee Judy would have looked so beautiful. Now that would have been a much more enjoyable Friday had it happened. He snored loudly as the dream led him to a beautiful beach where they could spend their honeymoon, lazing by the sea in their sun-baskets and dri nking   iced   coconut water from wee glass bowls. It all seemed so real until Daddy shook him and brought him back down to earth, ruining it all. During the dream, Wee Alfie had actually let off the most putrid smell which filled every orifice of the kitchen. It definitely didn't wiff of Wee Judy's rose-petal collar, that's for sure.

Within a matter of seconds Wee Alfie was out on his ear in the garden, helped by a hefty shove from his Daddy who still wore the shirt with the massive coffee stain that looked like a map of Africa, a stain that made the shove twice as hefty as it should have been.

'Oh, that's such a good one Daddy! You're ALWAYS blaming me, especially when you and Mummy have visitors for dinner and I'm mooching around their legs under the kitchen table hoping for a wee fallen scrap or two. It's 'Wee Alfie, you're stinkin!", when in fact it should me me saying, 'Ach Daddy, YOU'RE stinkin, my eyes are bleeding here'. (another reason for learning to talk, so as I can stick up

for myself) What are you going to use as an excuse Daddy when I'm not around and don't say Mummy cos she'll kill ya, although come to think of it, her's are the worst of all.'

He had managed a few sniffs along the garden path before stumbling across a cat in the bushes. Normally the cat would run for it's life as soon as it seen him and he would chase it, but not on this occasion. The cat purred, approached Wee Alfie with his tail in the air and Wee Alfie recognised him as the cat from Wee Judy's garden just down the road. By all accounts she and the cat got on like a house on fire and often curled up in the same basket on an oul cold winters evening. So it didn't seem right to scare it senseless and chase it back down the road seeing as it was such a close friend of Wee Judy's. The cat walked ever closer and its purr grew ever louder until they were almost touching noses, a bit of a first for Wee Alfie.

Wee Alfie's nose twitched as he caught the feint smell of roses. He sniffed the cat's ears and the fragrance became far stronger. Wait a minute, this was Wee Judy's cat-friend who had come to Wee Alfie's garden giving off the same beautiful scent of rose petals he had dreamt off before being kicked out into the garden by his annoyed Daddy. Had Wee Judy had the same dream at the same time? Was she trying to send a message to Wee Alfie via her housemate? Surely not. Things like that just didn't happen in real life. The cat rolled over on its back and playfully pawed at Wee Alfie and he responded by rubbing his nose along the neck and back of the cat. With that, the cat jumped off and raced back to Wee Judy, carrying the scent of Wee Alfie as he did so. She would now know that Wee Alfie had smelt the rose petals. Awwwwww, maybe dreams do come true after all. Many people say dogs don't dream or if they do they dream it's only in black and white. Who in the name of goodness comes up with such stupid conclusions. All dogs dream and they do so in full colour otherwise Wee Alfie would never have known that the rose petals on Wee Judy's collar were a beautiful shade of red.

He went back inside and Daddy locked the kitchen door. Instead of sleeping in the basket he made his way into the living-room where Mummy was taking a wee break from the social media and was reading a magazine. Things seemed really laid back as she dropped her hand down to stroke Wee Alfie on the head. He responded by laying flat out on his back on the floor, his favourite position for a belly rub. Daddy came into the room with two mugs of tea and a dog chew. He hoped the dog chew was for him and not Mummy, but with them pair, anything's possible. Things seemed all set for a nice lazy Friday afternoon, just like many Fridays before, until a conversation between Mummy and Daddy that made Wee Alfie sit bolt upright;

'Did you let Wee Alfie out?'

'Yes, he's been in the garden.'

'I thought so, but the really weird thing is we don't have any roses in our garden and yet Wee Alfie smells of roses. I just patted his head and my hand now smells like a flower shop.

'Strange, I don't think he ventured further than the garden.'

It would be true to say he didn't go any further than the garden fence and yet, within the last hour or so, he'd been to a sun-drenched beach with his best friend in the whole wide world. Wee Alfie, being such a clever talking dog, could have told them that, but he chose to keep quiet. It was none of their business where he'd been. As far as they were concerned he'd been to the shops that morning and that was good enough for him.

Wee Alfie settled down for his second long sleep of the day, obviously hoping he could pick things up from where he left off, but sadly that was not to be. He closed his eyes and before he knew it he was dreaming of upset babies screeching in his face with chocolate plastered all over their mouths. Dogs can't eat chocolate so Wee Alfie kept well away from them. He dreamt of what it was like to walk into a shop, how it would be to sit in the front passenger seat of the car for a change and not slung into the back like a spare anorak in case it rained. He dreamt of lots of things right through until Friday evening but Wee Judy sadly didn't appear again. He really wished Thursday hadn't ended as he so loved the romp in the park with the true love of his life.

Saturday

Wee Alfie woke up raring to go. Go where? Anywhere was the answer. He loved his Saturdays as much as he put up with Fridays because there was always something going on somewhere or other, something out of the ordinary. He loved the odd Saturday car boot sale for instance and this week his Mummy and Daddy had decided to head down there to see what bargains they could lay their hands on. They never saw anything they needed but still bought tons of stuff, thus confirming that one man's rubbish is another man's rubbish. Yes, one man's pile of junk is another man's pile of junk.

People say that a luxury is buying something you don't need at a price you can't afford, but it's a statement that would never be used to describe anything you'd get at a car-boot sale. It's generally full of rubbish you CAN afford that you definitely DON'T need. At least it was a chance for Wee Alfie to stretch the oul legs, although not too much or he would end up looking like a gazelle prancing about.

Wee Alfie often wondered why it was called a car-boot when he knew for definite that cars didn't wear boots. They had rubber tyres that didn't need to have pairs of boots slung over the top of them and logical Wee Alfie just didn't get it. He knew that would look just as stupid as his stretched legs. A car wearing welly boots indeed, I wouldn't think so.

But there's no flies on Wee Alfie that's for sure, well sometimes there is but only when he's had his nose stuffed into the rubbish bin. It's a bit of a dirty habit that he seems to enjoy despite his absolute terror of those nasty, vicious wasps. They think they own the place and aren't at all happy that others like Wee Alfie are prone to stickin their noses into something that belongs to them.

Just like the day before, Wee Alfie was flung into the back of the car and the three of them went off in search of a few rusty bargains in a great big guttery field. There's nothing a dog likes more than a field of pure muck, apart from perhaps a gravy bone.

His favourite stall sold doggie treats, things like pig's ears, disgusting in the extreme, and pretend slippers made from some weird stuff that had to be chewed for days on end until Wee Alfie nearly had lockjaw. They definitely weren't real slippers, the kind worn by his Granda, as they were a muddy puce colour and they didn't have that lovely smell of stinky socks or athlete's foot about them.

Wee Alfie, as logical as ever, always wondered about athlete's foot. Why didn't his Granda have athlete's feet in the plural, thus having the complaint on both of his feet instead of just the one. Surely if his Granda had only the one athletic foot, thought Wee Alfie, it would run a whole lot faster than the other one, meaning Granda would be forced to run round and round in circles, just like a great big eejit of a dog chasing its own tail. Wee Alfie had tried to do that just the once and was very disappointed with the outcome. He just didn't get that foot and feet thing at all. He thought humans had far more sense than that, if only he knew. He did remember a time when Granda had said to Granny that he was going round and round in circles, so he supposed that's what he meant.

Maybe he had one foot more athletic than the other. It made sense at last. Meanwhile, back at the car-boot sale.

On the upside his favourite stall always had loads of different biscuits, bones and chewy toys on offer, things that made Wee Alfie's eyes pop out on stalks. He remembered how this particular stall was right at the back end of the second aisle which meant walking past endless piles of junk that didn't interest him, or anyone else for that matter, in the slightest. Every car-boot sale he had ever been to had a mouth watering smell of burgers and hot dogs that filled his nose, making it twitch with expectation. The slabbers would be just trippin him. He didn't like onions though, rather he didn't eat onions because they were bad for him and other dogs too, but it was a lovely, wafting smell just the same and far more enticing than the piles of junk strewn all over the grass.

Mummy bought some tomato plants from a stall that was also selling a sump for an oul Mark 11 Ford Cortina and Daddy bought some oul vinyl albums by singers that had popped their clogs long before Wee Alfie was a twinkle in his Daddys eye.

To him it all seemed a bit of a waste of time bothering to look around, but he enjoyed the walk as he shook his head at the total rubbish people were trying to get rid of. There were more toys than Santa could ever carry on his sleigh and more second-hand clothes than would fit in all the wardrobes ever made in the entire world.

'That was actually one of the reasons why Mummy decided one day to load up the car and go and do a car-boot sale herself. Daddy had lost the plot a couple of days before that cos he was trying to get one of his shirts squashed into the wardrobe with no success. It was full to the neck of Mummys stuff, clothes she'd never even had on her back Daddy said. So at half six in the morning....I know, I didn't know that such a time even existed either, she headed off to the car-boot. She said she didn't even remember going cos she was still half asleep and drove there with one eye closed. Luckily for her the other one was still open. Daddy had said that it would do her good to have a good clear out. I know what he means cos when I go out into the garden for a

good clear out after great big feed, I definitely feel the better of it too.

So, she set up her stall and spent the morning arguing with the punters about the price of things. After a couple of hours she got bored and decided to go off and look at all the rest of the stalls...BIG MISTAKE. She bought all round her and ended up bringing more clutter home than she went with and had spent all the money too. Daddy was rippin and didn't speak to her for a good fortnight. I then became the middle man, in dog form, to help them when they wanted to communicate with each other. It was 'Alfie, tell your Mummy to pass the HP Sauce' or 'Alfie, tell your Daddy to get off his rear end and get it himself' etc etc.. I was wrecked by the end of it all. It was a full-time job and all I can say is thank goodness they're talking again so I can have a wee snore upside down on my favourite pouffe. '

Wee Alfie never stopped once to check out any of the items because it encouraged miserable looking stall-owners to glare down at him with their big scary gubs on them. Maybe they thought he would wee on their boxes of unwanted books or CDs, as if Alfie would do that! The stall of house plants, yes probably, but definitely not the books and CDs. They all looked ready to give him a swift boot up the backside and so, no, he didn't hang about. A car-boot up the road was one thing but a boot up the rear-end was something else altogether.

There was another stall that sold ridiculous dog-leads as well as jigsaws with pieces missing and buckled garden tools that had seen better days. He hoped Mummy wouldn't notice the stupid pink things with attached collars that were covered with little flashing lights. Honestly, can you imagine what Wee Alfie's mates would make of that if they saw him strutting round the park looking like a multi-coloured ice-cream van. They'd be queuing up for a poke with a big flake in it, if only they were allowed chocolate. He definitely would have fitted in perfectly at an Elton John concert. No, he really did hope Mummy would miss that stall and, to make sure she did exactly that, he wrastled on the lead to get her attention as they approached it. It worked a treat. Not a doggie treat sadly, just a treat. She roared at him and Wee Alfie just wagged his tail with relief. No treat in the offing but the distraction had definitely done it's job.

'Mummy's always buying me stupid embarrassing things to wear like wacky jumpers, bow ties, luminous raincoats, cool vests....the list is endless. Oh how they all laughed when I turned up at my Granny and Grandas with the full Christmas regalia on including socks with bells on and a pair of reindeer antlers. Well, it was the middle of July. No, seriously now, loads of photos were taken so that even more people had the opportunity to take their end at me. Thank goodness for small mercies, at least Wee Judy didn't see them. The only thing to do when wearing one of these shockin items is to sniff out the smelliest substance you can find and roll in it. Sometimes that doesn't work out too well for me though cos I'm not the best at rollin in stuff. I can find it all right but my aim isn't great and if you're not quick enough and don't hit it first time, Mummy as you whipped away from the area pretty sharpish with a dislocated neck to boot. So I guess I'll just have to wear it and bear it.'

By lunchtime Wee Alfie was well and truly wrecked. There's an awful lot of stopping and starting for a dog at a car-boot sale and this particular Saturday was no exception. There were loads of other dogs there too always trying to attract Wee Alfie's attention because he was so famous now. He was sure that one of them actually had a Wee Alfie tattoo on its front leg but that was nothing more than Wee Alfie acting the big man and getting way above his station.

He was done out as he fell into his basket for a midday nap. He closed his eyes and tried to forget the luminous pink lead with the flashing lights. Oh for goodness sake, who on this earth would buy such a thing for their pet without the risk of being ate alive? His Mummy wouldn't because, thankfully, she hadn't seen them on display. A tip for any dog owners, such a lead and flashing collar may look nice on a French Poodle but I wouldn't risk stickin one on a Bulldog if you want to keep your legs.

Having said all that it was an interesting stroll for Wee Alfie, something different for him away from the usual run around the garden or gallop round the park. As an added bonus he never once had to go and fetch a stick thrown by his Daddy, which at times did get a bit tedious. Sometimes he had to bring the stick back more than a dozen times before his Daddy got fed up with the game, not realising Wee Alfie was sick to the back teeth of it after only the third throw.

It isn't the same for them Australian dogs it has to be said. They never have to waste their time playing that stupid game because their owners throw clever things called boomerangs that know how to come back on their own. Wee Alfie envied them Australian dogs that just lazed about on the beach watching their owners polish off half a dozen cans of lager while their pets lay upside down sunning themselves. They never had to chase anything other than the odd half a sausage chucked on the ground at a beach barbecue.

He woke up and wandered into the living-room to find his Daddy glued to the television. Not literally of course, nobody does that literally, I don't think anyway, but Daddy just loved his sport and Saturday was THE BEST day to watch it, especially today because his favourite game, the rugby was on. What in the name of goodness is the purpose of rugby? A fair enough question thought Alfie. It seemed to him to be just a big field full of blokes in their summer outfits rolling about in the gutters fighting over a ball. Surely in this day and age, they could afford a ball each? Alfie also thought that they were in need of some kind of anger management training. Nevertheless, Daddy just loved the game, hardly surprising though as he definitely needed some kind of anger management training of his own, particularly if Wee Alfie had a bit of an accident on the lovely polished floor. Daddy always roared and shouted when he was watching sport on the telly and he wasn't even playing. How did he expect them to hear him when they were miles away? Sometimes Alfie just despaired. Apparently, rugby is a very ancient game by all accounts and goes way back to the days when The Dead Sea wasn't even sick. That's maybe another reason why his Daddy liked it, cos he was really really old.

Wee Alfie spent the Saturday afternoon snoozing at his Daddy's feet, ignoring the shouts at the telly, while Mummy did something or other in the kitchen, she not being a rugby fan. He loved that snooze because Saturday evening was always his favourite dinner of gorgeous mince stirred into gravy as thick as garden muck, so he had something very special to look forward to. Oh how he loved it and he loved to be wide awake and refreshed to enjoy devouring his big delicious feed. It made him break wind more than other meals during the week though, but he put that down to excitement and satisfaction rather than the actual meal itself. So although the rugby had caused a bit of a stink in the afternoon in the living-room, Wee Alfie caused much the same in the kitchen that evening. Once again, as on previous days, Daddy and Wee Alfie were quits.

The meal was as delicious as Wee Alfie had expected, a real treat. Daddy didn't say too much as his favourite team had got stuffed during the afternoon tussle but Wee Alfie couldn't have cared less. He had a belly that was fit to burst which he knew would drag along the ground when he went out, but sure it had been well worth it. It was different when snow was on the ground but that wasn't the case today thankfully.

If it wasn't sport on the telly then it was a film. Wee Alfie had no problem with that unless the film starred Lassie the wonderdog and that brought on pangs of terrible jealousy. Wee Alfie had always fancied himself as a bit of a movie star, so much so that he invented films and tried to convince other dogs that he had starred in them and was in fact THE top actor in Colliewood. For instance, there was Star Paws, Home Alone As Usual, The Bodyguard Dog, Jurassic Bark, Marley and Wee Alfie, One Dalmation, Free Wee Alfie, The Great Dane Escape, the list went on and on until the bored doggie listeners had drifted off to sleep. If any dogs were still awake he'd tell them all about the authors he had co-written best-sellers or great poems with too, such as J.K.Growling, Virginia Woof, Wee Alfie Lord Tennyson, Terrier Pratchett, another ridiculous list that also went on and on.

It was almost time for bed when Daddy opened the kitchen door and ordered Wee Alfie and that overladen belly out into the garden. He nearly jumped out of his fur when an owl, yes a huge owl, swooped by at such a low level, like a fighter plane and it nearly took his head clean off. Owls weren't seen too often in back gardens in Northern Ireland and the length of its wings were frightening to one as small as Wee Alfie. The heart was racin out of him and he barked his head off to try and scare away the giant beast. He'd never seen an owl before, only ever hearing his Mummy and Daddy slabberin about the more famous ones like Owl Capone or Owl Pacino, and he was relieved when the bird swooped, circled a couple of times and made its way to the garden next door in search of a mouse supper, a fine example of a take-away. Wee Alfie laughed to himself when he realised that most things screech to a halt suddenly but owls screech when they take off, and they're supposed to be wise? Not wise more like. So how come then that they did such a simple thing round the wrong way? Owl come? Haha! Do you get it?

What with all the barking from Wee Alfie, Daddy, still not in the best of moods, called him back indoors for fear of annoying the neighbours and he settled into his basket for a nice dream that would take him into Sunday morning. Maybe Wee Judy would turn up in his dream. He lived in hope as he closed his eyes. He loved to dream of being a singer if he couldn't be a movie star. He had his favourite songs that he growled away to as he nodded off. There was Hello Doggie, songs from Annie Get Your Gundog, Daydream Retriever, Mutt of Kintyre and Bulldog Blitz.

Mummy and Daddy switched off the lights and the house was in complete darkness. Nobody or nothing could see anything at all, nothing could possibly see anything in such darkness apart from an owl, it once again getting things the wrong way round and it had long gone with the take-away in its beak. Goodbye Saturday. Sunday would be a completely different ball-game altogether.

Sunday

Wee Alfie woke up on this bright Sunday morning to the sound of church bells ringing in his ears, well it was either that or a serious attack of canker that had spread from his mouth. He always had a wee lie in on this very special day of the week, just like his Mummy and Daddy. It was their one last chance to enjoy a bit of luxury before the new week began.

The day always started the same with Daddy taking Alfie on a wee dander down to the local village shop to collect the Sunday papers and today was no exception.

'To be honest, one of the main reasons why I love Sundays so much is that I get to walk to the shop and don't have to get into the car with them pair. It's always worse when Daddy's driving. It's nothing to do with anything he does, it's Mummy, she's the world's worst passenger. Everything that Daddy does when he's driving isn't right..

'Watch that kerb, slow down, are you stickin to that speed limit?'

It's constant. He can't even look out of his own eyeballs properly to please her. They have a car each so I don't understand why they have to get into the same one to be at each other's throats all the time. The next of it will be 'Could you stop breathing cos it's really annoying'. That wouldn't end well, where would you be then Mummy? Who would put the bins out or red up all the scraps off your plate at tea time? I'm up for that one if you're stuck. Daddy just needs to remember to take the bins back in again cos that was another shouting match, as the bags of rubbish for the whole week were piled up on the patio. You'd think he'd learn his lesson. It wasn't so bad for me though cos that was another thing for me to pee on.

It's Daddy's job to cut the grass too and he absolutely hates it, especially when he accidentally drives over some of my recycled food. He shouts words I've never even heard of before and that aren't good for my wee delicate ears. Even though he hates grass cutting, he's all proud of it when it's finished and he always says 'Would you look at that, it's like a bowling green'. Well I'll tell you what, I wouldn't be paying to play on it cos it's up and down like my back leg on the way home from the shop. He also has one of them big petrol strimmers and he loves using that for wacking down the weeds. He's even offered to do Mummy's hair with it but she wasn't that keen for some strange reason. It couldn't look any worse than it does now, in my humble, or not so humble, opinion.

Mummy fell out with him last week cos he went a bit mad with the oul pruning shears. She went out to have a look at his handiwork and couldn't find the plum tree. He'd cut it down to the quick. Apparently he'd thought it looked a bit uneven and he kept cutting and cutting until eventually there was nothing left. Plum crazy it was. He got another stripe took off him for that one and she ate the bake off him. Good job he has a thick skin and knows how to handle Mummy. He says that the best thing to do is just say 'Yes dear' and everything she says must go in one ear and out the other. Anything for a quiet life.'

Loads of others seemed to have had the very same idea as them which meant that Wee Alfie was tied to a post outside the village shop along with two other dogs whose owners were also pretending that they were excellent readers too. He'd seen both of them dogs before and so it wasn't much of an issue for him. Yes, there were a few awkward sniffs and snuffles and a bit of tail-wagging but nothing as nasty as he'd have got from Buster the angry Bulldog if he had turned up. There wouldn't be much of a chance of that though because if his owner was anything like Buster, reading newspapers would be way down on his list of priorities, even though he probably couldn't even spell list.

His Daddy didn't buy a newspaper on the other six days of the week, but the Sunday read was a tradition as indeed it was for many other dog walkers. He turned immediately to the sports pages when he came out of the shop, reading the reports on the various sporting events that had taken place the day before, so Wee Alfie had to sit and wait a while for the return journey home. He was totally bored out of his scull. There were very disturbing headlines on the front page, a story about a natural disaster in a far away place that Wee Alfie had never even heard of, much further away than Cork, but Daddy skipped all the big, important stories and went straight for the back page as was usually the case.

He untied Wee Alfie's lead from the post and they finally set off for home. You would think that his Daddy was both old enough and ugly enough not to try and read a newspaper whilst walking along the road, but no, you guessed it, he walked straight into a lamp-post in true Laurel and Hardy style. It was all a bit embarrassing for Wee Alfie as Daddy stumbled around like some oul drunk on his way home from the pub. Passers by were giving him dirty looks and some even crossed the road to avoid him.

By the time they had almost reached the house he had a massive bump on his noggin the size of a tennis ball. If he were able to, he would have ripped it off and slung it down the garden for Wee Alfie to chase. That would be the type of him all right. All joking aside, it looked like he'd grown another head, or at least as if one was well and truly on its way.

Wee Alfie had heard people say that two heads were better than one and that may well be the case under certain circumstances, but two heads on his Daddy's one body really did look stupid. Tweedledee and Tweedledum sprung to mind, well actually it sort of did but Wee Alfie had never really heard of them before so that image didn't hang around too long in his grey matter.

When they finally made it home, in a zig-zag fashion, Mummy tended to her wounded man as he told her how Wee Alfie had bolted off after a stray cat and how he'd saved Wee Alfie's life at the very last minute by diving in front of a passing car. How brave, Mummy's heart was bursting with pride. She believed every mumbling, bumbling word (the big eejit) and looked at Alfie with raised eyebrows and a shaking head of disbelief and disappointment. He'd been a very naughty boy indeed, even though he really hadn't. Daddy gave him a sideways glance out of the corner of his eye, a different kind of glance, one of apology and with a wee sneaky wink attached. Wee Alfie wasn't too bothered either way though. Deep down, Mummy knew that he had more sense than to run out in front of a speeding car. Having said that she had also thought Daddy had a bit more wit than to try and read a newspaper and walk home at the same time. Oh dear, why was it all so confusing on this ordinarily simple Sunday morning.

Another Sunday ritual was Mummy giving Wee Alfie's basket a good oul clean and brush out, getting rid of all the doggie hairs that had shed off him during the week, (it's surprising he's not bald by now really) along with bits of chewed up toys and gravy bone crumbs. She sprayed it with something or other which made it smell like a portaloo and for the rest of the day he thought it was best to sleep beside the fire away from the stinkin waft of chemicals. So at the moment he wasn't so much Wee Alfie as Alfred The Grate. Mummy hung the basket on the washing line in the garden along with a few flowery blouses and various more delicate pieces of frilly clothing that only saw the light of day when the washing was hung out. Put it this way, it was stuff only Mummy wore and definitely not Daddy EVER.

By dinner time Daddy's second head had expanded into an eye sore as well as a head sore and he felt well and truly as miserable as sin. A nice wee trip out and a long dander to follow had been previously planned but it didn't look too likely now as Daddy's bump kept changing colour like a set of traffic lights. One minute it was black, then purple and by the time Mummy had peeled the spuds it was more yellowy, not exactly the normal colour of traffic lights it has to be said, but near enough.

'Sunday dinner is another one of my favourite meals of the whole week. I find it really strange that Mummy and Daddy only have Sunday dinners on a Sunday. They're really gorgeous so there should definitely be more, maybe every other day.

I have my paws crossed that Mummy will do roast potatoes instead of them boring plain boiled ones. They're far far tastier although Mummy reckons that they're really fattening and the last time she made them she said, 'Alfie, you needn't think you're getting any cos you're fairly puttin the beef on'. I thought to myself, Mummy, did you ever hear of a saying that people in glass houses shouldn't throw stones? My Mummy throws boulders, she certainly does. She is forever on some sort of diet or other. There was the cabbage soup diet, the no carbs diet and the worst of the lot, the boiled egg diet. Daddy wasn't keen on that one I can tell you, although at least I wasn't blamed for the obvious for a nice change. But these diets never last and she only seems to stick them for a lock of days and then she's back to gorging herself again.

Every Monday morning after a big piggin out session over the weekend it's always, 'I mean it this time, I'm disgusted with myself, it's back on the diet for me'. I just roll my eyes and think, aye right Mummy. Anyway, what's wrong with a wee bit of paddin, sure it keeps you insulated especially coming into the winter and Mummy wouldn't need the half of them clothes in the wardrobe. She could flog them all on Ebay, make a clean fortune and the two of them could retire to the Bahamas. I'll stay here cos it would be too warm for me. I still maintain that a wee bit of everything wouldn't do you a button of harm, well, apart from things like onions, chocolate, grapes and all them things that dogs aren't allowed. It's not fair, them two can eat everything, and they do, on a very regular basis. In January, straight after Christmas in case your geography isn't too good, the dieting goes clean off the scale and Mummy wouldn't even lip anything sweet. It might go on for a week or so until she can't stick it any longer and out comes the great big family size bar of chocolate which is inhaled (no time is wasted on chewing at all). I for one am very thankful that you eat like a pig Mummy cos it means you have a lovely spongy knee for me to lie on. I'd hate a bony Mummy, so keep stuffin your face.'

The usual Sunday procedure was Mummy prepared the vegetables, put them in a wee pan of water to soak for later and then they would set off in search of somewhere new and exciting to visit. Daddy surprisingly turned out to be a real trooper and instead of hamming it up like Mummy did when she smacked her toe on the kitchen cupboard the other day, he insisted he was feeling better and fancied a bit of a breath of fresh air. There's loads of beauty spots to choose from in Northern Ireland, much nicer than the thing on Daddy's head which was more like a large bump than a spot, but a beauty just the same.

The planned trip took the three of them to the Giant's Causeway in County Antrim, right up on the north coast at the very top of Ireland, a bit of a drive in the car but an awful lot quicker than walking according to Wee Alfie. For those who have never been there it's listed as the fourth greatest wonder in the United Kingdom, the fifth if you include Wee Alfie's favourite butcher's shop that sells the juiciest bones on all of this earth. Legend goes that the Causeway was built by a giant by the name of Finn Mc Cool, a giant name, who was about to knock the living daylights out of another big giant from Scotland. To Wee Alfie it was a bit like Gullivers Travels, on rocks that happened to be shaped like fifty pees. The main thing for him was that he was at the seaside again for the second time in the one week and that made it very special indeed. He wasn't too keen on clambering over so many rocks as it hurt his delicate wee paws, but the beauty of the place was a sight for sore eyes.

A big tall man with an Alsatian was far braver than most and Wee Alfie watched the pair of them clambering around like arrogant mountaineers, as sure footed as a couple of Irish dancers. Yes of course he hoped for the same as you would have hoped but it never happened. Sadly, they climbed down safely, killing some of the fun out of the day.

It had been a fantastic trip breathing in the bracing fresh air and coastal smells, all new to Wee Alfie.

The journey home took a considerable while but Wee Alfie slept most of the way, there was nothing else he could do cos he didn't have a driving licence. Mummy and Daddy had enjoyed the wee jaunt out too, so much so that they sang their hearts out for mile after mile. Oh how Wee Alfie cursed the broken radio as he would much rather have listened to the Shipping Forecasts than all that wailing. Back home again safe and sound, Wee Alfie spent a while in his basket picking various bits and pieces out of his paws, including an ancient fossil that looked a little bit like the woman next door and then he fell sound asleep.

Daddy had a bit of a shiner the next day but luckily hadn't sprouted another head. At least that was what Daddy thought until he went to the doctor's and the receptionist told him AND his bump that the doctor could only see one patient at a time. And so it was that another week in the life of Wee Alfie had begun.

Alfie's Special Days

Well there you have it, a week in the life of Wee Alfie. Lots of happy times, meeting lots of other dogs, lots of disasters and accidents involving his Mummy and Daddy, accidents that made Wee Alfie snigger under his fur, all part of a normal week in such a strange Northern Ireland household. But Wee Alfie has enjoyed many very special days too, not in this particular week, but throughout the year and probably the greatest day of his whole life was when he got a Valentine's card from his girlfriend Wee Judy. That day is always in his list of specials, right at the very top.

He wasn't expecting a Valentine's Card last February, of course he wasn't, what dog would? He saw the postman approaching the front door and he was all set to have a good oul bark and a bit of a snap when the postie waved the envelope at him;

'Don't you snap at me, Wee Alfie, I have something very special in my hand for you,' said the postman.

Alfie stood back, he didn't know what the man was on about. He hadn't done any online shopping and he definitely hadn't been done for speeding, he never ran fast enough around the park to get a ticket.

'I don't know who this is from but the envelope has a beautiful smell of flowers.'

The postman had never really tried to speak to a dog before in the belief it would understand and respond in some way, but hey, there's a first time for everything and, let's be honest here, he definitely chose the right dog didn't he?

He didn't know too much about the secret skills of Wee Alfie and so he was knocked clean sideroads when Wee Alfie forgot about the barking and trotted calmly over to sniff the envelope. It did indeed smell of roses and Wee Alfie knew exactly who had sent the card.

'It's Valentine's Day, the very day when you send a card to someone who you are fond of,' continued the postie.

Wee Alfie wagged his tail, it had to be a special message from Wee Judy. It certainly wasn't a threatening letter from Buster the Bulldog. Wee Alfie didn't know anything about cards on Valentine's Day, neither did his Mummy who had only ever had one and that was the one she sent to herself, she could tell that from the handwriting. Daddy always told Mummy he would have sent her a Valentine's Card but he didn't have her address, a strange statement as they'd been married for five years when he said it. He once gave her an envelope pretending it was from him but when Mummy opened it was actually a final demand from the electric company. Oh how she laughed at that one, NOT.

Wee Alfie burst into tears. He couldn't believe he'd had such a wonderful card from Wee Judy and it made for a very special Valentine's Day indeed, made even more special when Mummy paid the electricity bill and stopped the house being plunged into darkness. Who needs a dozen red roses when you have light?

Wee Alfie waved goodbye to the postie as he walked down the path, promising he would never bark or bite him again.

You would think Wee Alfie would have thought of his birthday as a special day but, unfortunately like other dogs, he hadn't a clue what day he was born. Owners tend to make up dates of birth for their pets, apart from people who keep tropical fish in an aquarium. What a nightmare that would be, nipping down to the post office every day to buy a fistful of waterproof cards for a shoal of neons and a Japanese Fighting Fish.

Wee Alfie never even got so much as an ordinary oul birthday card let alone a nice gravy cake with candles on top. Imagine going through life and never blowing a candle out? Now if that had happened that really would have been a special day for Wee Alfie. He would just love to have blown at candles until he blew something stinky out the other end.

That's about it as far as Wee Alfie's special days are concerned apart from the one time he peed on Buster the Bulldog's leg without him noticing. Mind you, if he had noticed it wouldn't have been just a special day, it would have been his last day ever. But Wee Alfie lived to fight another day. That was a special day, the day he realised he could look after himself whenever he got himself in a bit of a tangle. No more worrying about owls or seagulls, or even floating crisp packets. If he could take on Buster the Bulldog then he could handle absolutely anything or anyone in the weeks that followed. Don't worry, there won't be a new book every week, even though Wee Alfie is set for so many more adventures.

Thank You

When I first started to write my books, I thought to myself, I'll never be able to think of anything to say but then it was pointed out to me that I was definitely a bit of a slabber. Mummy and Daddy says I could talk for Ireland. Well if that's the case, them two have the rest of the entire world covered.

The main thing that helps me write and slabber is to know that I have all of you, my brilliant friends supporting me in my efforts. Thank you all from the bottom of my doggie heart for sending me all them lovely messages and pictures of your furry babies actually reading my books! I'm surrounded by a big new doggie family and I love you all, but don't tell Wee Judy. However, much as I love you, I just need to get one thing straight right now before we go any further, I won't be buying you all presents at Christmas or on your birthdays, but I promise to think of you with great fondness on them special days. If the presents I get are anything to go by, you should count yourself lucky you're not getting any. So, thank you for buying my book (that's another box of Gravy

Bones for me!) and hope you have a good oul read. Lots of love and great big slabbery licks,

Wee Alfie x

Printed in Great Britain
by Amazon